MW00414687

Merry Christmas!

A.G. Reidy

CONTENTS

Preface

Gary

Ridley Field

Mrs. Morris

My First Naked Woman

Rupture

S.Y.P.

Whistling Pines

Clown

I Call the Fat

A Halloween Story

The King

Let's Dance

Boom

St. Louis

Mick

Gramps

I Nailed It!

The Carson Sisters

Snow Days

Pastor James

Hopelessly Devoted

Epilogue

We were younger then…

take me back to when.

—*Ed Sheeran, "Castle on the Hill"*

This book is dedicated to my siblings. This is

where it all started.

Just "the *five* of us!"

PREFACE

Let me start out by saying some of this book is inappropriate. It is *not* politically correct and it may offend some people. It has stereotypes and comments that were used during the time it was set. It also has bad words and speaks of naughty deeds. You might not want to let the kids read this. If you are easily offended or don't have the ability to laugh at adolescent, boy humor, then *dinkweed* probably won't be your cup of tea.

Consider yourself warned.

Now that I have that out of the way, let me tell you a few other things.

First, I'm a hack. I don't pretend to be a great writer. I write like I play the piano. I know enough for it to sound like a song, but I won't be playing any concerts. I've been told that I can tell a pretty good story though, so hopefully this will translate well on paper.

Second, every story in this book has a thread of truth running through it. I changed names, combined characters, and have taken poetic license throughout each story. But every chapter contains a bit of truth. Those who know me and my family may recognize a story or a character. I make no apologies. How can you apologize for truth?

Next, I want to dedicate this book to my brothers. Life would have been boring growing up without my three dinkweeds. They were the humor in the house, the opinionated big mouths (my sister and I are the same—we all get it from Dad!), and loyal to a fault.

They have given me so much fodder for stories that I didn't need to include my sister and myself as much. Although a few of the stories are our own, we play more of a background role. To be honest, we are just not as interesting as my brothers are. In spite of it all, even having to deal with the teenage-hormonal-angst, my brothers made life fun.

It was obvious to me early on that one of us would have to take pen to paper and record these stories, so I grabbed the chance first. I couldn't make this crap up.

I'll never tell which brother did what or if I've combined the stories of my brothers with the stories of my neighbors. Some are my own stories. Others may be stories I heard secondhand. I'll keep those details secret.

Also, while you read this, remember that this is being told through the eyes of a fourteen to sixteen-year-old boy, not a fifty-something year old woman!

As for my brothers, I love them all. They are upstanding, creative, honorable men and wonderful husbands and fathers—each with their own talents. Luckily, all of them have never completely let go of their dinkweed status. I hope they never do. Life is fun having each of them in it.

So these are the stories, in no particular order. Enjoy!

GARY

Throughout my teenage and adult life, I've had a reputation for being a bit of a "dick!" I wasn't bothered or surprised by this title. If I'm being honest, there was some truth to it.

Being a bit of a dick helped me keep people at an arm's length because they didn't know how to read me. It was okay that way. To be honest, I think it gave me an air of mystery.

But I wasn't a dick all the time. As the oldest of three brothers, I also played the part of protector and defender. My job was simple. I took care of my brothers and beat up anyone I had to on their behalf. My two brothers, Aaron and Michael, looked up to me like I was a god, the keeper of the keys, and the ruler of the kingdom. If the three of us were anything like the *Three Stooges*, I was the Moe of the group. The King Stooge. They thought I knew everything, and believe me, I played that up big time. For every question they had, I had an answer—real or made up.

"Why does the bridge hum every time a car goes over it?" my brother Aaron asked from his bunk bed.

We were in our shared bedroom, lying in the darkness on a warm summer night. The window was open and I listened to the bridge hum for a minute before answering him.

"Simple," I said, "don't you know about the bees?"

Of course, he didn't know anything about the bees because I was making it all up on the spot.

"There's a bee colony under that bridge, hundreds and thousands of bees, and every time a car drives over it, it disturbs them and they hum and buzz. Be really careful walking over that bridge. One slip or loud noise and they'll fly up and sting you to death. They've done it before to little kids like you. There's no death so painful."

For years after I told Aaron this story, Ma would ask why he'd walk the long way over the Bridge Street Bridge and not the humming bridge on his way home from work. He told her it was good exercise, but I knew he was full of shit. He was afraid of the bees.

We lived in a small neighborhood in the city of Lowell, Massachusetts. Sitting on the edge of the

Merrimack River, Lowell is home to many historical mills. We're also known for some great celebrities like Jack Kerouac, Ed McMahon, Bette Davis, and Mickey Ward.

Like every other city in the world, there are rich sections and poor sections. We lived a step above the poor section. For the most part, we had a pretty decent life. We lived on a street with single-family homes and a few tenements. These single-family homes were what put us one step ahead of the poorest parts of the city. It was a neighborhood full of stay-at-home mothers and fathers who worked hard and drank hard too.

My Old Man wasn't around much during the week. He'd bust his ass all day working as a parts man with a diesel truck company, come home and eat dinner, suck down a Schlitz, and head back out to wash the floors at the local nursing home.

Dad grew up in Dracut, Massachusetts during the time when most people still considered it the country. He had three brothers and a sister. He grew up poor, but loved, in a house his father built.

Dad was a paratrooper during The Korean War, and he fought in The Battle of Outpost Harry, which I've heard is a pretty big deal. He had a reputation of being a tough son-of-a-bitch, someone you wouldn't mess with, but lucky for us kids, most of the toughness we saw was in his yelling if we pissed him off. This wasn't hard to do.

He wasn't a hitter though. Not like some of the other dads. We had it easy in that regard. I had one buddy, Rick, who once busted out a window when we were playing stick ball. The next day his eye was swollen shut and purple. He said he fell going down cellar to get something for his ma but we knew his dad more than likely beat the tar out of him. Rick's dad was a mean drunk.

Ma grew up in Lowell in a decent home with three sisters, a brother and a lot of aunts that my grandparents would take in until they found husbands (some never did). She was English and beautiful. With her more privileged upbringing, she and Dad were different in that respect.

Dad used to tell a story about the "Lowell Bums" who would ride their bikes to Kenwood in Dracut.

Dad told us how he and his brothers would throw rocks at them and tell them to go back to the city. He used to joke and say that the bikers were actually Ma and her girlfriends.

Ma met Dad for the first time at a dance. She said he was handsome with dark brown eyes, which was a contrast to her bright blue eyes. He asked her to dance. He had warm hands and he was quiet. The second time she saw him was downtown at the five and dime. They ran into each other and he asked if they could have a cup of coffee, and then he walked her home. He told her he wouldn't marry her until he found a good job. The story in the family is that she replied, "who said anything about getting married?"

Since then, they've been Dan and Carole together. Three boys later and living in a house of their own, life wasn't too bad. Growing up in Lowell was something Ma was comfortable with, and Dad got used to being a "Lowell Bum."

I liked it here too, but you had to be street smart. When you lived in a neighborhood like I did and you were the type of guy I was, you had to pay attention to the little things that others didn't notice.

Sometimes this came in handy, and other times it would creep you out.

It came in real handy one time when I spotted my neighbor, Mary, catching some rays on her short roof.

People living in the city didn't have much space or a yard to speak of. Going to the beach was nothing more than a nice daydream. Usually, the lots had a slab of asphalt on the side of the house that was too hot to walk on in the summer. The tar would get mushy and blistering hot, and no bullshit, your feet would burn if you were barefoot. Some lucky people had a backyard, but it was little more than a strip of grass to throw a few flowers in. So what yard you did have, your other brothers or sisters played in. But if you had a short flat roof, that became your beach! Most of the girls in the neighborhood, as they got older, liked to lay out and catch a few rays on those roofs. I liked to watch them do it.

This was how Mary Martin usually spent her days during the summer. The Martins and their two daughters, Mary and Angie, lived next door.

Mary had big cans.

14

One day, while Mary was enjoying the sun and I was enjoying the scenery, I noticed that Arthur, the pimple-faced dweeb from the next street over, was also enjoying the scenery. I could see his beady eyes through the slats of the blinds in his room directly in line with the roof Mary was on.

This pissed me off for more than a few reasons. First, if I was gonna choose any girl in the neighborhood to be my girl, it'd be Mary. So, technically this douche was boning on my girl. It also pissed me off because he was interrupting my own bone-fest.

The good thing was that he couldn't see me. My brother, Aaron, rigged our blinds in such a way it was hard to tell when we were looking out the window. Aaron said he did it to "spy on the neighborhood." I knew he was too young to be into girls, so he was just watching people do everyday things. *Little dinkweed!*

Arthur, on the other hand, was a bully. Of course, he never picked on Aaron or Mike though. As most of us know, a bully and a pussy go hand in hand. He was afraid of me so he didn't mess with my brothers.

I sat there peeking through the corner of the blinds, with one eye on him and the other on Mary's ample jugs, trying to think up a plan. *What to do? What to do?*

Then I remembered my father's black box.

Dad had a black box he kept next to his bed. It contained a few scratch tickets he hadn't scratched yet, a date book, a couple of letters Ma wrote him when they were dating, some army metals, a half bottle of Jack, and various weapons he had confiscated from us. Like my sling shot.

I snuck in Dad's room, opened the box I wasn't supposed to know about, took a swig of Jack, and grabbed the sling shot. This would do just fine.

Taking a few crystal rocks out of the vase with the fake flowers Ma kept on the desk in the hallway, I retreated back to my room and peeked out the window. First at Mary, to confirm that she was still there with her glistening, sweaty boobs. Then, over at Arthur. He was still there, and I could only see one of his hands. I had a pretty good idea where the missing one was! I felt my blood boil.

I loaded up the smooth crystal rocks in to the sling shot, aimed, and fired with the precision of David going against Goliath. He had his window opened, but the slated blinds were pulled down. Like something out of a movie, it went straight through the slat he had opened to watch Mary, and *boom*! I caught him right in the eye!

He screamed loudly, "SHIT!!! OOOwwwwww, what the *fuck*!" And Arthur, with one hand over his eye, pulled the blinds right off the casing as Mary jumped up. It wasn't hard for her to put two and two together once she saw Arthur tangled up in the blinds and holding his eye.

"What's going on! Were you watching me?" she screamed.

He stumbled and mumbled something I couldn't hear.

"You're a friggin' pervert! I'm telling!" she screamed again as she grabbed her towel and climbed through the window yelling for her mother.

I pulled up the blinds on my window. The movement caught Arthur's eye and we made eye contact.

A look of understanding came over his face and he said, "hey, did you do that?"

I smiled, gave him the finger, and walked away.

I heard him yell after me, "*what a dick!*"

My mission was accomplished, my dick status intact.

RIDLEY'S FIELD

Growing up in the city, we were always on the lookout for places to play.

There was a florist shop at the top of our street with an empty lot next to it. It had all the things a typical empty lot had: overgrown grass, wildflowers, and a few trees on a big hill.

Living in the city, this lot was the only patch of country we had, and we played there year-round. In summer, we played hide and seek, army, and Relievio. In winter, we slid down the hill on old pieces of cardboard.

A few years ago, a young boy died in a horrible train accident, and they dedicated the lot to his memory. He had been playing chicken against the train. He lost. When they found his body, he had been knocked right out of his sneakers. And so, Warren Ridley would forever be attached to that vacant lot.

Warren was an okay kid. He was one of the regulars who played in the field with us. Most people liked him. All except Mary's little sister, Angie.

One winter night, at his suggestion, Angie fell for the "lick that frozen pole" trick, and Mary had to help pry her frozen tongue from the pole.

"Warren, you are the biggest therk I ever met. You're dead to de!" Angie screamed with a lisp as blood ran down her mouth.

Afterwards, Warren felt bad about it all, and caught up with Mary.

"Hey, Mary! Really, I'm sorry. I didn't know the damage would be that bad. Please tell Ang that I'm sorry," he said.

"I'll pass it on, Warren," Mary said as she walked away.

That was his last winter in the field with us. Come springtime, Warren started hanging out with a rougher crowd and we didn't see him much after that. Rumor had it there were problems at home. His mom and dad were breaking up, which was pretty uncommon to hear about in the early seventies. We heard that Warren was taking it hard.

A small part of me wondered if Warren had maybe fallen in front of the train accidentally-on-purpose. His dad left his mom after that and she became a heavy drinker.

After Warren died, Mary told me that Angie felt bad she had never talked to Warren again after the tongue-stuck-to-the-pole incident. What Angie didn't say was that it kept her up some nights wondering if the last thing she said to him, that he was dead to her, had been a curse. We all carry a bag of hammers in life, that would be in Angies.

Warren wasn't the only thing Ridley Field is remembered for though. It's also where I touched my first, almost naked boob.

It all began during our usual game of Relievio. Relievio is this neighborhood-wide, hide-and-seek-tag game with a home base. When you were caught and put on base, you waited to be relieved by your teammates. Sometimes, if it was taking too long, you'd yell out, "BA, HA, HA, HE, HO" just to let your team know you were caught. *Stupid, I know, but looking back, so was the way we would all sing-song a friend's name on their front steps instead of just knocking on the stupid door when we wanted them to come out.*

We had finished splitting everyone up into two teams. As one of the captains, I made sure that Shelly from the next street over was on my team.

Shelly had big cans and she wasn't shy about it. She never wore a bra either even though she should have. Her mother refused to buy her one, and she still wore t-shirts. Don't think this escaped my notice when I was picking my team. Shelly always had an eye for me, and I always had an eye for her cans.

Since I won a game of rock-paper-scissors with Mary, who was the other captain, my team got to hide first.

I stuck with Shelly. As we laid in the tall grass *hiding*, I moved my index finger up to my lips and said, "shh, we just need to lie here quietly until they find us."

After waiting a moment, I leaned forward and kissed her. She tasted like the Swedish Fish our team had eaten while we discussed our game strategy.

She French kissed me, just like she had all the times we'd played Spin the Bottle in Lance's cellar. I lifted my hand and laid it on her waist.

Okay, I thought, *it's now or never*.

22

I slowly moved my hand up and laid it on her boob. Shelley's breath caught, but she didn't try to push me away. I gently squeezed, and felt a cushy, pliable mound underneath her t-shirt.

After a few squeezes, I decided I wanted to touch it naked. Again, I moved my hand back to her waist; I waited a fake respectable moment, and then slid it under her shirt. I felt her little smooth stomach roll and inched my way up. Shelly rolled slightly onto her back to give me a better angle. She was accommodating that way. I inched my hand up. I felt the bottom crease of her boob, I knew that I only needed a few more inches until I'd be at the nipple—

"GARY, YOU *DICK*! Way to not play the game, we were captured and stuck on base waiting for you two to come and save us. You took so long that everyone got sick of waiting and went home! What the hell are you two doing?" Michael screamed at the top of his lungs.

Shelly jumped to her feet and said, "I'd better get home. Ma will be looking for me."

As I felt heat rush into my cheeks, I turned to Michael and calmly said, "I'll give you to the count of

23

three until I ram my fist into your fucking face. One, two—"

Michael bolted back home before I could get to three.

As I lay there waiting for my fourteen-year-old erection to subside, I thought, *next time I'm cutting the outside feel and going straight for the nipple.*

MRS. MORRIS

Mrs. Morris was our eighth-grade music teacher. She looked like a white version of Mrs. Evans on the show *Good Times*. She had blondish, short, tightly-curled hair and very broad shoulders. But unlike Mrs. Evans, she was from the south, very *loud*, and she had a terrible temper.

She used to get in our faces and scream at the top of her lungs, with neck veins bulging, "LITTLE MISTER, WHY DON'T YOU JUST SHUT YER MOUTH?" It was a rhetorical question. Answering the question would have pissed her off more and we would have regretted it immediately.

We never sang a lot of songs in her music class. Instead, she had us practice square dancing. The dancing would usually start with Mrs. Morris singing, "allemande left and swing your partner round and round," but usually ended with "do-si-do......I SAID DO-SI-DO, ARE YA DEAF?" She'd scream with spit flying.

One afternoon, she came in and told us we were going to do a variety show.

"Isn't that a fun idea, children? We will do it like a gong show *type-of-thang*."

"That's stupid," I heard Arthur mutter.

"STUPID? STUPID! I'll show you stupid! You will be stupid and mute when I'm done with you, little mister! DO YOU HEAR WHAT I'M SAYING TO Y'ALL!!!" she screamed through gritted teeth. She gave a whole new meaning to TMJ.

"Y'all will do it and like it. DO I MAKE MYSELF PERFECTLY *CA-LEE-ER*?"

So, we had a week to come up with our skit for the show. She told a group of eighth graders to think of a talent on their own and offered us no help or suggestions. This further reinforced how insane she was in most of our minds. The plan was that we would get on stage next week for our first dry run.

On Monday morning, during first period music class, a group of twenty-one not so bright-eyed and bushytailed eighth-graders filed in ready to reveal their talents.

I was a genius. While walking into the music room, I sauntered up to Mrs. Morris and said in my

26

best kiss-ass voice, "the color of your sweater looks great on you, Mrs. Morris."

She smiled a big toothy grin and drawled, "why you little rascal—take your seat."

After attendance, I immediately raised my hand and said, "excuse me, Mrs. Morris, I was thinking that for a production such as this, we really should have someone in charge of sets and back stage. I'd like to volunteer my services."

"Why that would be gentlemanly of you, Gary. JUST DON'T MESS UP," she yelled the last part because she couldn't help herself.

I was officially off the hook! I could get away with doing as little as possible. More than a few of my friends were pissed they hadn't thought of my brilliant idea. While they worked on their performances and talents, I sat in the back of the auditorium and pretended to take notes. I was lucky that Mrs. Morris never looked over my shoulder as I wrote—she'd scream herself hoarse if she saw all the boobs and dicks I doodled on my "notes."

Margaret was up first. She wore a red Bozo wig left over from Halloween and a matching red dress. I

27

thought that this first act seemed promising. She sang a dramatic rendition of "On the Good Ship Lollypop" that Shirley Temple sang in a movie. She looked like a moron, but that was okay because Mrs. Morris liked it. I heard her mutter, "now we are getting somewhere."

It all went downhill from there…

Next up was Mary and three of her friends. Mary stood and sang "Old McDonald," while her three friends (on their hands and knees) played the parts of the animals. I only really cared because I had a nice view of cleavage from where I sat.

Mrs. Morris hated their performance. She yelled, "LADIES, WHAT THE BLAZES IS THAT? If I had a *GONG* I'd bang it! It probably took you all of five minutes to think that up! Get off the stage and improve your performance."

One act after another kept on a steady course of decline. Matt played a very bad tin whistle version of "Danny Boy" that only a dog could hear. Maria tried to play the spoons but kept dropping them.

But the last straw was Ray-Ray.

Ray-Ray was a bully and a little nuts. When he came out on the stage and said he'd like to perform "The Star-Spangled Banner," I saw the surprise on Mrs. Morris' face. She smiled and said, "FINALLY an act we can be proud of! That would be nice, Ray. Let's hear it."

Ray-Ray obliged. He cupped his hand, put it into his shirt, and played "The Star-Spangled Banner" with armpit farts!

Needless to say, Mrs. Morris called the show off shortly after that.

Years later we found out that in the ten years that Mrs. Morris was the music teacher, every year she planned to put on a big show, but there never was a single one.

A few years later, I heard that she went to jail in a domestic violence incident a few years after she retired. Her husband tried to shoot her in self-defense. No big shocker there!

MY FIRST NAKED WOMAN

Frank lived two houses down the street from me. He was Twenty-two, and too cool for school. Literally. He dropped out of school in his freshman year, took some under-the-table construction gigs, and never looked back.

Frank was a character. The only time he seemed to have pants on was when he was going to or coming home from work. I imagined the moment he walked into his house; he'd take them off and throw them in a ball in the corner.

He liked to watch us play our games with the other neighborhood kids. He'd stand on his front porch, with one hand in the waistband of his boxers, smoking a butt and shake his head at us. Like he couldn't believe what morons we were.

Sometimes, when he was feeling generous, he'd interrupt our game and offer up some pearl of wisdom. More often than not, it was to tell us that we weren't following the rules of the game and he'd take it upon himself to enlighten us while insulting our intelligence.

"Hey idiots! It's Duck-Duck-*Goose* not Duck-Duck-*Ghouls*. Jesus H. Cripes."

It was a typical, lazy afternoon that found me and a few of the guys hanging in my yard, drinking Coca-Cola, and making plans for how we'd spend the day. We kept going back and forth between getting a group of girls together to play Spin the Bottle in Lance's cellar (his mom was at work) or going to the local pool to spy on the girls in their bikinis.

Then, Frank came out of his house and interrupted our planning. He stood, a few chain-linked fences separating us, and looked at us. He was dressed in his usual attire (boxers with a butt hanging from his mouth).

After taking a few long drags, he called out to us, "hey, ball sacks, any of you boneheads ever see a naked woman?"

We all looked at him trying to figure out why he was asking and how we should respond. Should we tell him the truth, which was a resounding "no?" Or would we be better off making something up?

Frank lost his patience before any of us could answer and said, "I'll ask again, and don't lie because I'll know. I can smell it. *Any of you Bozos ever see a naked woman?*"

I spoke up after a few more moments of silence. "nah, wish I could say I had, but that'd be a lie." With that, all the other guys chimed in the same.

He took another long drag on his butt, flicked it, and said, "come around to the side door. Keep your mouths shut. One loud noise and I'll pop you one."

Curious, but not knowing what was going on, we walked over to his yard. Frank waited for us at the side door. He put a finger to his lips and said, "shut your mouths and follow me."

We followed him quietly into the house in a single-file line. Frank led us to a room off of the kitchen, and he again put his finger to his lips and shushed us. He opened the door.

There, lying on the bed and sound asleep, bare-assed and buck-naked was Margie!

We all heard Frank bragging about how he went out once in a while with an older woman. At twenty-five, Margie had three years on Frank, as well as a reputation of being free and easy. She wasn't bad looking with her blond hair and blue eyes. She was a little thick around the middle, but she had a nice rack.

I felt my mouth drop open. We all stood there staring. I started at her head and slowly lowered my gaze wanting to take it all in. My eyes made their way down to her boobs, hovered there for a bit, and then made their way to the Holy Grail. The first thing I noticed, was that the carpet did not match the drapes. Her giant pubic bush (remember it was the 70's) was brown, which confused me a little. I could see the other guys were confused and red in the face.

Even so, it was a sight to behold. We stood in the doorway and gawked for a few more minutes until Frank ushered us out.

When all four of us got back outside, with four boners I'm sure, Frank stuck his finger in each of our faces and said, "if you idiots ever open your mouth about this, and if it ever gets back to me, I'll fucking kill yas! *Got it?*"

We all swore up and down we'd zip our lips. And we did. We never even talked to each other about it.

From that day on, whenever we saw Margie walk by we slowed down and stopped what we were doing and stare, stuck in our own reverie. I bet we looked like idiots with a far off look on our faces. Afterwards, we'd all give a silent thank you to Frank and an even more silent apology to Margie.

RUPTURE

If you're sliding down a rope and your balls start to smoke, that's a rupture.

If you're sliding into base and your balls hit your face, that's a rupture.

If you fall on a dock and your balls hit a rock, that's a rupture.

If you're running down the street and your knees beat your meat, that's a rupture.

These were a few of the "*rupturisms*," if you will, that my brothers and I came up with the summer we found out Kyle Cote got a rupture.

None of us knew what a rupture was other than it had something to do with what my Ma explained as your "nether region." Which meant nothing to us until Dad mouthed "*your balls*" at us behind her back. We all cringed at the same time.

Kyle Cote's ruptured balls were a hot topic of conversation among us for hours afterwards. We were discussing it when Frank stepped out on his porch dressed in his boxers with a butt hanging from his mouth.

"What the fuck are you morons talking about?" he asked across the yard. "I heard someone say balls."

Aaron blurted out, "Kyle Cote has a rupture and Dad said it has to do with balls."

"Do you know what a rupture is?" Michael asked.

"Yes, I do numb-nuts, it's when your nuts bust outta your ball bag. Fuckin' hurts like a bastard," he said.

We sat there feeling sick to our stomachs trying to wrap our brains around that visual. Seeing our reaction, and that he had our full attention, he went on, "my cousin, Weezer, got one from moving a refrigerator. Nut popped right outta his ball sack. Never saw anything like it in my life," he ended the last bit in a whisper and his eyes got a far off look in them.

"Anyway, you imbeciles, if you can get a peek at Kyle's bag, you won't believe it. Well, I'm done shooting the breeze with you dinkweeds. Got better

36

fucking things to do," he said as he flicked his cigarette away and went back inside his house.

"*Wow*, that's friggin' gross. I can't even imagine," Michael said with a greenish tint to his face.

"I never want to. I could puke just thinking about it," Aaron said.

"So, how are we gonna get a look at that sack?" I asked my brothers.

Each of us had a plan that would get us into Kyle's house and a way to get a look at his bag. None of the plans were any good. There was something missing…

"Angie!" I burst out.

Everyone in the neighborhood knew Kyle had a thing for Angie. He didn't do a good job hiding it. Whenever we played Catch and Kiss in Ridley Field or Spin the Bottle in Lance's cellar, Kyle would puff up whenever he had the chance to kiss her. We had no idea whether or not Angie felt the same, but she didn't bitch too much when she had to kiss him and she always went red in the cheeks. So, maybe she did like him.

After some careful thought and conversation, I came up with a plan. The next day I stopped by Kyle's house with a get well soon card. Mrs. Cote answered the door in a bathrobe and hair rollers. "what'cha want, Gary?" she asked holding a lipstick-stained Camel cigarette in one hand.

Putting on my best fake caring voice, I answered, "Mrs. Cote, I just wanted to come by and tell you how sorry we all are to hear about Kyle's surgery. I was wondering if you wouldn't mind giving him this card we all signed?"

She coughed and tried to clear the soupy phlegm out of her throat and said, "well, that's really nice, Gary. Kyle is resting now, but I'll be sure to give him the card."

Off I went. I knew when Kyle opened the card, he be excited to see that everyone had signed it, including Angie. In reality, I forged everyone's signature. The key to this plan: A little P.S. about something I needed to tell Kyle about Angie.

As soon as I got home, there was a message waiting for me from Kyle asking that I stop by for a visit after school tomorrow.

38

The trap was set and the bait was in place.

My brothers—scared, disgusted, and morbidly curious—told me they would fink about the card if I didn't bring them along for the ball viewing. I had no choice but to bring them with me. The little pricks learned from the master.

The next day, we arrived on the Cote's porch exactly ten minutes after school let out. I told my brothers to let me do all the talking. I knocked and Mrs. Cote opened the door. She was still smoking a Camel cigarette, but this time she was dressed in a lilac, polyester pantsuit and her hair was up in a Priscilla Presley bouffant doo.

"Hello, boys, let me bring you up to Kyle. I want no shenanigans. He can't over exert himself, okay?"

"Absolutely no problem at all, Ma'am," I said in my best fake sincere voice.

She showed us to Kyle's room and told us, "fifteen minutes boys. That's it!"

We slowly walked over to Kyle.

"Hey, man. Are you okay?"

"Yeah, I'm alright if I don't move around too much," he said.

Kyle was covered in a thick blanket with only his feet exposed. He wore these fuzzy ankle slippers.

"Why the heck are you are you wearing princess slippers!" Michael yelled.

"Shut the hell up," Kyle said, "they aren't slippers they're heel protectors so I don't get bed sores or some shit like that."

"Oh okay" Michael said, "I thought you were turning fairy on us because you busted your nuts."

I reached over and smacked Michael in the head. The moron! Although, truth be told, I was close to busting a nut of my own trying to hold in my laughter. Kyle seemed pleased that I put the kybosh on the smart-assed remarks.

Wasting no time on small talk, Kyle steered the conversation to what he really wanted to talk about.

"Hey, man. What did you mean by that note you put in the card?"

"What note?" I asked, playing dumb. I wanted him to squirm a little.

"The note about Ang!"

"Oh right! That note," I said. "Well we told her you had surgery. We explained everything to her and she seemed very worried and concerned. She wanted to know if she could come see you."

Kyle struggled to sit up, "wait! You told her the real reason I had the surgery?"

"Yeah, I did. She is very concerned and wanted to make sure you're okay."

"Wait, wow! Really? She's concerned? *Wow!*"

"Do you want me to tell her it's okay for her to stop by tomorrow? Would ya like that?"

"Would I ever! Yeah!"

"Okay, buddy. I'll let her know. You have my word," I promised.

After a few more minutes of buttering him up, I went in for the kill, "hey, since we're here and everything, why don't ya show us how you're healing up!"

"Geez, Gary. I don't know…I mean it's my nuts and stuff."

"Aw, cut the shit man! We've been in the same gym class three years in a row—what d'ya got to be embarrassed about? Geez, we're like brothers." *I was really laying on the bullshit.*

"Well, I mean, I never thought of it that way! Okay. But remember, it's still healing and the swelling still has to go down."

After a few seconds that felt like minutes, Kyle pulled down his blanket and lifted up his johnnie.

Aaron and Michael recoiled in horror and jolted away from the sight of the bloated, revolting bag that was the size and color of an eggplant. They stumbled back as though they thought it had teeth and would bite them.

I sat on the bed and said, "what the fuck, brutha! Are you sure that will go back to normal?"

Kyle pulled down his johnnie and said, "awww, come on! It's not that bad. At least it's not leaking anymore."

Aaron and Michael both started gagging and ran from the room.

"Well…okay, bud," I said, "I'll be seeing ya."

Kyle reminded me to tell Angie she could visit him the following day.

The next morning, I went to our bathroom medicine cabinet and grabbed the cream Dad used to take care of the dry skin on his hands. Ironically, it was called *Bag Balm*. Then, I headed out to Angie's house.

I found her sitting on her front steps reading and drinking lemonade.

"Hey, Gary. What's up?" she asked looking up from the *Archie* comic book she was reading.

"Hey, Ang, did you hear about Kyle?"

"No, what's going on?" she asked concerned.

"He had surgery on his lower leg. He's okay, but now he's bummed out because he's stuck in bed all day. I know it'd cheer him up if you stopped by to say 'hey.'"

She perked up, but still seemed doubtful, so I set another trap, "it's no lie, Ang. We all know Kyle is a little sweet on you."

She blushed and said, "well, I'd be lying if I didn't say I was a little sweet on him too!"

"Great, when you go and see him, you can help him out by massaging his leg. It's the only way to make it feel better. I was going to head over to help him out with this cream, but why don't you go instead?"

43

With that, she took the cream and headed to Kyle's place. I walked away with a big smile on my face and I said over my shoulder, "don't forget: Be cheery!"

I heard later that Angie had burst into Kyle's room and told him very brightly and *loudly,* "HEY KYLE, IM HERE TO CHEER YOU UP! I'M HERE TO RUB YOU DOWN WITH THIS BAG BALM. C'MON, LIFT THE COVERS! THIS SHOULD MAKE YOU FEEL REALLY GOOD!"

Kyle lifted, Angie fainted.

She didn't talk to me for two months afterwards!

S.Y.P.

It was the usual Sunday routine that we had whenever a New England sports team was playing that day with Dad. Ma always made us snacks before she left to go visit Aunt Marie down the street. Dad would have a can of beer, and we'd drink Coca-Cola out of a cold, glass bottle.

This particular Sunday was no different. It was warm and sunny, and the windows were thrown wide open. We could hear all the city noises and smell the asphalt heating up. But none of that mattered—our focus was on the game.

Especially today when the Red Sox were playing against the Yankees!

Aaron started the conversation in his usual way, "hey, I have a question for you." We all knew what that meant. Aaron was *that* kid who always asked the hypothetical, would-you-rather, who-would-win-in-a-fight questions.

Michael hated these questions. He never saw the point in thinking about something that would never

45

happen. However, he would always end up answering just to shut Aaron up.

This time, Aaron asked, "if you could have *any* superpower, what would it be?"

This was no small question. This was the kind of question I liked. I wasn't interested in the questions girls always enjoyed asking. You know, those ones about *hair styles* or *bell bottoms versus gauchos*. I liked these no-bullshit questions that took some thought.

So, did everyone else. We sat there thinking. And then Dad started to smile.

After a few more minutes of silence, Dad said, "youngest to oldest—Aaron you're first. Name your power and what you'd do with it. At the end, we'll vote about who has the best superpower."

Aaron thought some more and then said, "I'd be super strong. I pick this power so that when my brothers or anyone else in the neighborhood messed with me I could mess them up before anyone even noticed. One small squeeze of my hand would break fingers. One flick of my finger would snap a bone. One tap of my toe would knock them on their butts!"

We sat there awhile to consider this. Then Michael shared his super power.

Michael was the most practical and logical of us. He never said anything without weighing all his options. He was a big planner. He's still like that to this day. There is nothing impulsive about Michael. I was almost sure he'd ask if we could play this game tomorrow so that he'd have more time to think. He didn't though.

"I'd want to be able to fly. If there was an earthquake, I'd lift my feet off the ground to avoid any problems. If there was a tornado, I'd whisk high above the clouds until it was over. If someone was trying to kick my ass, I'd fly away."

Again, we mulled his choice over. And then it was my turn.

"Invisibility. I'd be able to see who was talking about me, and then I'd know who I couldn't trust. I'd also sneak into Mary's room and watch her get undressed—sorry, Dad. And I'd sneak into the teacher's Rec Room and hear what they talk about when there are no kids around. The possibilities are endless."

Again, we all sat in silence—except for Dad. He gave a chuckle and sat there with a big smile on his face.

"Dad, why the smile? Have you thought about your power?" I asked.

"I didn't have to just think about it. I've known my entire life," he said.

"Your whole life? Quit holding out then—let's hear it!" Michael said.

Dad pointed his finger out and arched his thumb to make a gun symbol and pointed it at us. "S. Y. P!" he said.

"What's S.Y.P?" asked Aaron.

"Well, it ain't 'Say Your Prayers!' That's for sure," Dad said with a laugh.

"Come on Dad. What's it mean?" I asked.

"SHIT. YOUR. PANTS" said Dad.

"Think about it," he continued, "if someone cuts you off in traffic, S.Y.P! You ask your boss for a raise and he says no. As you leave, you whisper a quiet S.Y.P. You ask a broad out on a date, she acts too good for you and says no. S.Y.P! No one would ever mess with you again, *ever*. It'd get to the point

48

where you'd just point and all your problems would end there."

Dad put his hands behind his head, leaned back in his chair, and smiled at us. Pleased with himself and said, "*well?*"

Mike, Aaron and I sat there with our mouths open and imagined the possibilities. I thought to myself, *if I had that power the day I caught Arthur jacking off to Mary on her roof I would have given him an S.Y.P.*

A million different scenarios were running through my head. After a few minutes, we all looked at each other, nodded in unison, and said, "YOU WIN!"

Dad just smiled and said, "naturally."

As the Red Sox continued their battle against the Yankees, I thought of how I could make every one of those Yankees become Stankees with one point of the finger and an S.Y.P! If only...

WHISTLING PINES

My folks always saved just enough money to take us to away for summer vacation. I'm not sure how they managed it, but every year we packed up and drove way up to the mountains of New Hampshire.

While the rich kids in the city spent their summers at Hampton Beach or Cape Cod, we traveled three hours through the boonies to a place called Bethlehem. Even though it wasn't the most exciting place in the world, we couldn't bitch about it because we were one of the only families in our neighborhood who could afford to take a vacation at all.

We went to the mountains because Ma said she liked them better than the ocean. There probably was some truth to that, she wasn't a lay out at the beach type-of-gal, but I know the price had a lot to do with it. For half the price of the beach we could get a nice cabin at Whistling Pines.

Ma also preferred the mountains to the beach were there were no girls for me to bone on. No chicks strolling the boardwalk in their bikinis. It was a favorite vacation destination for pasty, old ladies and their husbands.

Truth be told, we didn't miss the beach a bit. Michael and Aaron were too young to think about the girls, and there was enough to do there that it didn't bug me too much. Ma used to let me bring my cousin, Billy. So, that made up for it.

Billy was my partner in crime and my smartass twin. We were both kinda dicks and loved a good prank. Especially at the expense of my brothers.

We were able to get the good cabin the same week every year called Cherry. Cherry had two floors, a fireplace, a spiral staircase, and it was right on the edge of the lake.

There was one bedroom downstairs and Billy and I called it every year. We would feel like bachelors living on our own down there. It even had its own entrance that we imagined using as a way to sneak chicks in. We never did, but it was nice to dream. We'd discuss in length how we'd have a signal to give each other if we were inside having sex and needed privacy. It never entered the conversation that my parents and brothers were just upstairs.

The lake at Whistling Pines came equipped with a paddleboat and some row boats. Next to the lake, there was a heated, kidney-shaped pool for chilly nights and an unheated pool for warm days.

There was also a roped off area of the property that didn't have cabins. Instead, there was a row of motel rooms. It was where the Hasidic Jews stayed. Whistling Pines was a favorite vacation place for them too.

The owner told us, "that part is Kosher—stay away if you aren't Jewish!" Believe it or not, we never went past the rope. We figured something bad would happen if we did. A few times Billy and I hid on the side of the motels and peeked through the tall grass, hoping to see something, but we never did.

There was also a small restaurant right on the property called Sadie's Diner. We all saved our allowance a month before vacation so we could get breakfast at the restaurant one of the days we were there. Michael and Aaron liked to go to breakfast by themselves, and I usually went with Billy one day.

Billy and I decided to go to breakfast the second day we were there. We felt very grown-up eating breakfast on our own without my pain-in-the-ass brothers or parents.

The scrambled eggs were so light and fluffy, they looked like clouds floating on the plate. We also ordered a side of crispy bacon and baked beans, and we washed it all down with a hot cup of joe.

After adding a third spoonful of sugar to his second cup of coffee, Billy said, "I have a story to tell ya."

It went like this. His mom, my Aunt Marie, took him to get a Tetanus Shot the week before. In the waiting room he sat next to this mother and her three-year-old son. She told Marie in a panic that her son was pooping bright green, and that they were waiting on the results of a stool sample she brought in to the doctor that morning. *Stool means shit, Billy clarified.*

She got called into the office right before Billy did. As luck would have it, on Billy's way out they saw the woman and Marie asked her, "what was the outcome of the sample?"

The woman said, "you won't believe it, they ran a test and turns out he got into a packet of lime Jell-O. It was just Jell-O—can you imagine?"

"Well, oh-my-goodness. I never would have guessed!"

As Billy was riding home with his mom, he kept thinking about how lucky he was to have gone to the doctors that day.

This got me thinking. While we finished up the last of our coffee, we hatched a plan.

Billy pulled out a box of lime Jell-O from his pocket. He came prepared—I tell ya: Great minds think alike. "The way I figure it, if I down this now and have a big lunch, I should be ready for a nice and steamy turd by two o'clock," he said.

Without wasting anymore time, he downed the Jell-O mixture like it was powdered candy.

After breakfast, we decided to take a spin on a paddleboat to iron out the details of our plan and to talk about chicks before lunch. I told him about how I almost touched Shelley's naked boob, and he agreed with me about the threat I made to my brother.

"That little muthafucka! He killed your horny and stopped you from getting nipple."

He told me he that never got to touch a nipple, but he saw one of his sister's friends' once. She was taking a shower at his house after a sleepover and he "accidently" walked in as she was getting out of the shower. Although we both knew it was more of an accidentally-on-purpose thing. He said her nipples were pink, that's what he remembers most. She screamed as she covered her lower privates but he saw her nipples. He apologized then spent the next hour whacking off in his bedroom.

"Oh well," he said, "maybe one day we'll both get lucky and get more than a peek."

He asked if I'd ever got to see a real nipple, and I lied and said I hadn't. I was too afraid to fess up about Margie. Even up here on the lake, I didn't want Frank or Margie finding out.

We spent the rest of the time on the lake seeing how many bull frogs we could find. We put a red X

55

on their backs with marker to keep an accurate count before we tossed them back in the water.

As we made our way back to the cabin, we were surprised to see that Billy's folks, Aunt Marie and Uncle Ronnie, had decided to come up for the day. They were having a beer on the porch with Ma and Dad.

Marie was Ma's sister, and they always had a lot to talk about. They would sit and gossip for hours about everyone and everything.

"Did you hear Betty Cook called me last week?" Aunt Marie asked. Then without waiting for an answer, she continued, "she found lipstick on her husband's collar just like in the detergent commercial. He told her an 'associate' gave him a greeting kiss and that's how it got there. '*Greeting kiss, my behind*,' I wanted to tell her."

They always "wanted to tell someone something" but everyone who knew my Ma and Aunt Marie knew neither one of them would say shit with a mouthful.

Dad and Uncle Ronnie were funny. They could sit for five hours and not say one friggin' word to each other, and then later they'd talk about what a swell time they had. It was odd, we knew they must have liked each other, especially Dad who wouldn't sit with anyone for more than five minutes if he didn't like them. I once saw him stand up after spending a minute with someone, look at Ma, roll his eyes, and say in his most dick-ish voice, "well I gotta go." And then he upped and left while the poor guy was in the middle of a sentence. He never did this with Uncle Ronnie. It made Ma happy because her and Marie were close and it meant they could spend more time together.

As we climbed the steps of the porch, the first words out of Billy's mouth were, "hey, Ma, hey Pop, I'm friggin' starving! I need a real, real big lunch," he said and winked at me on the side.

Before Uncle Ron could say anything, Dad piped up, "Billy, don't say that word in front of your mother. It's offensive." *If that ain't the pot calling the kettle black!* After Billy apologized, Ma jumped up and said she'd throw on some burgers.

Billy asked for two, and then he leaned in and whispered to me, "I wanna get a big turd going."

Ma asked me what was so funny when I started to giggle and I just shrugged. She gave me a weird look as she walked away.

After lunch, we decided to lay on the double hammock near the lake to catch a snooze until it was time to execute our plan. We slept head-to-feet, 'cause it would'a been gay to sleep face-to-face. As an adult, I realized that this reasoning was ridiculous because our dicks were still lined up next to each other. At the time though, it made sense. We both ended up snoozing for a little over an hour.

I woke to Billy nudging my foot, "wake up, Gar, quick! I don't want to shit my pants."

We jumped up to find my brothers. We told them sometime after lunch we'd take them down to the trout pound. This was reasonable because that was the one area Ma didn't want them going without me. "Safety in numbers," she would chant. We grabbed them and told them to get their fishing poles, and we all made our way down to the pond.

As we stood at the water's edge, we talked about the cool things we'd do for the rest of the week.

Billy, according to our plan, said, "hey guys, did I ever tell you I have a kinda magic thing I can do?"

"What magic thing?" asked Aaron.

"Well, don't ask me how I do it 'cause I have no friggin' idea—but if I concentrate hard enough on a color, I can make my body shit that color."

"BULLSHIT!" I yelled. "No one can do that. It's impossible."

"Are you calling me a liar?" Billy shot back.

"Well, I don't think you can either," Michael said.

"Say that again and I'll knock you on your ass! Why would I make something like that up?" Then he said in a dramatic voice, "I'm kinda hurt, guys—my own cousins—that you would accuse me of lying about such a thing."

Mike felt bad and said, "gee Billy, you gotta admit, it sounds unbelievable. I mean, who could do that? I'm sorry. It's just that I have never heard of that."

Aaron chimed in, "not to call you a liar, Bill, but I still don't think you can do that."

Billy's gaze fell to me and I said, "BULLSHIT."

"Okay, I'll prove it to you all. For a price! Ten bucks! Ten bucks says I'll let you guys pick a color, and if I shit that color, I get the money," Billy said.

"What if you don't shit that color?" Mike asked.

"Well, I'll take the money from my paper route for the next six months and pay you all back. Eleven bucks each! A buck in interest to you all."

"Gee I don't know, Billy," said Aaron, "I only have 10 bucks for the week as it is. You'll take my restaurant money."

"Me too," Michael said.

"I'm so sure you won't be able to do it that I'll take that bet," I said with conviction.

"You think he's bluffing, Gary?" asked Mike.

"I'm sure he is," I said.

"Listen guys, I gotta shit! So, are we doing this or not? I gotta start concentrating on a color *now*!" Billy said frantically.

As Aaron and Mike hemmed and hawed, I said, "I'm in. I pick green!"

60

"Okay, whoever isn't in doesn't get to see!"

That was the push the boys needed, they couldn't stand the thought of me getting to be the only one who could see it.

"I'm in!" Aaron shouted.

"Me too," said Mike.

Billy walked over to the side of the road. He closed his eyes tight and said loudly, "Think green! Green peas, green trees, green leaves, *all things green*! Come on, body! Don't let me down!" When he started to rub his belly and wiggle his hips, it was all I could do to not start laughing.

"Okay, I think I'm ready now. Please, no talking. I need quiet to concentrate as I shit."

Then he dropped his draws and proceeded to crap on the side of the road. When he was done, he grabbed a handful of leaves and wiped his ass. He walked away without looking and said, "someone take a look and tell me."

Aaron ran over and I saw his mouth open wide. "*What*! I can't believe this! Guys, come here!"

We all walked over cautiously. Sitting on a pile of leaves was the brightest green turd I had ever seen.

"I would have never believed it if I didn't see it with my own eyes!" said Mike.

"Geez!" I said.

We all walked back to the cabin in silence.

After Billy collected his money from the boys, we changed out of our jeans and put on our bathing suits. We wanted to swim to celebrate a perfectly executed plan. While we swam, we decided we would have a victory breakfast with our winnings at Sadie's again the next morning.

Ma and Dad weren't too happy about the bet. Ma seemed mostly disgusted, and Dad shook his head and called us dumbasses. We never mentioned the Jell-O.

At seven o'clock the next morning, we ran out of the cabin and over to the diner. We were surprised to find Dad, Ma, and the boys already there and eating breakfast. We were more than a little pissed off.

"What are you guys doing here? *Not fair*! Billy won a bet and they still get to have breakfast in here?" I hissed.

"Don't get mad at us, guys, Dad offered. What were we gonna say? *No*?" said Mike.

"You never take us here. This sucks. You should pay for me and Billy's breakfast too!" I bitched.

"I will not," said Dad, "shut up, take your winnings and go sit at another table."

I figured I better quit before I really ticked Dad off. We sat at our own table, but our breakfast didn't taste as good as it should have. Dad never gave *me* any freebies.

At the end of the meal, we headed to the bathroom to take a whiz. As we entered, we saw Dad drying his hands with a paper towel at the sink. Before he left the bathroom, he came up and stood behind us and said, "boys, when you are done in here come back to the cabin. There are chores to do."

"Chores! Dad, give us a break. This is vacation," I said indignantly.

"Yeah, I know it's vacation, but there are still chores to do and you two will be doing them."

"We never had to before," I said.

"Well, you will now. We all gotta pitch in. Just this morning, Ma had me go around the cabin and collect all the dirty clothes you kids throw around so she could do laundry."

He paused, and then continued, "it's funny the stuff you find when you clean out pockets."

As I zipped up my fly, I saw Dad reach into his back pocket and pull out the crushed lime Jell-O box.

He walked up to Billy and put the box on top of the urinal he was standing at and said, "I'll have a list of chores waiting for you both at the cabin." And then he left.

We stood there with our mouths hanging open. I looked at the crushed Jell-O box and then I looked at Billy. After a few seconds of this, Billy started laughing out loud and said, "that son-of-a-bitch outsmarted us!"

Billy and I spent the remainder of the day doing all of Dad's chores while he sat on the deck drinking his Schlitz and chuckling. At one point, he toasted us as we walked by and said, "you can always count on a peckerhead to trip himself up. It's a mathematical certainty."

He took a long swig of beer. "It's a good vacation, boys. A good vacation."

CLOWN

One summer afternoon, while I sat in Dad's chair and enjoyed an episode of the *Flintstones*, my brother Aaron walked by me dressed as a clown. He wore a big, red wig, a nose to match, and baggy clothes. In his hand, he had a bulging, paper lunch bag. Ma yelled at him from the kitchen, "okay, sweetie, are you going now?" Aaron told her he was and he walked out the door.

"Gary, I need you to go follow your brother," Ma said from the kitchen doorway.

"Follow him! Ma, I'm busy! What the heck for?"

"Gary, *PLEASE*," she said with urgency. Ma sounded almost frantic now. "He saved his allowance for two weeks and bought penny candy with the money. He wants to go hand it out to the kids in the neighborhood. You have to follow him and make sure no one makes fun of him or gives him a hard time."

"Dressed as a clown! Are you kidding me? Of course, they'll make fun of him. Not to mention it's creepy as hell!" I said indignantly.

However, right after I said it, I realized it would be a good thing to have Ma owe me for later.

"Fine, I'll go," I said while thinking, *what a dinkweed this little shit is.*

When I got to the gate I saw Aaron half way down the street. He was standing at the fence of the Foster's house. They had two little girls and I saw them take candy out of his bag. All smiling. If Aaron wasn't a young kid, I could see some of the parents calling the cops about some weirdo dressed as a clown giving candy to their kids. Instead, Mrs. Foster stood at her front door and smiled at the scene.

As Aaron continued his walk through the neighborhood, I figured I'd keep some space between us. I didn't want to rain on the little peckerhead's parade.

The sign of trouble came when Kyle and Ricky turned the corner and saw Aaron. They started to laugh, but before they could get a word out, I raised my fist at them from behind Aaron's back. Even though these guys were my buddies, they'd get a pop from me if they made my little brother cry. I had no choice. It was the Code of Brothers. I could call him anything I wanted to, and make him cry even, but if anyone else did that, they'd have to deal with me.

After about half an hour of Aaron sharing his bag of candy with all the little kids in the neighborhood, he turned to make his way back home. I was leaning up against a fence as he walked by. I acted like I had just been hanging out and I asked him what he was up to.

"Why the clown costume?" I said.

"I don't know," he said, "I just wanted to share some candy with the little kids around here. Half of them don't ever have money for Mr. Softee or get an allowance like we do, so I thought they might like a treat."

I put my arm around his shoulder, and we walked the rest of the way home. *Maybe I'm more of a clown sometimes than Aaron was.*

When we got home, Ma was happy to see it all went well. When Aaron left the room to get out of his costume, Ma let me know how grateful she was that I had kept an eye on him.

Perfect, now to execute my plan, I thought. "Hey Ma, ya know how I have a birthday coming up at the end of the week? How 'bout me and you take the bus on Saturday morning over to Sears. Maybe I can find something there to pick out for my birthday. Wanna do that?" I asked.

"Gary, that would be nice. I'll ask Grandma to keep an eye on your brothers and you and I can do that. I have a few dollars for you to pick something out."

Nothing makes a mother happier than spending some quality time with her kids.

That following Saturday, I could barely contain my excitement as Ma and I waited for the bus.

"What do you have in mind for your present Gary?" Ma asked as we found our seats.

"I'm not sure, but I'm sure when I see it, I'll know right away," I lied.

As we rode to Sears, I put my arm around Ma and smiled.

Not missing a beat, she said, "what are you up to, you bugga'?"

"Not a thing, Ma. Just glad to be spending time with ya without everyone else around."

69

This wasn't a complete lie.

My first mistake when we arrived at Sears was holding her hand and rushing to the back of the store. Upon reflection, I should have meandered a bit, like we just happened to stumble upon that section. As soon as we arrived at the gun counter, I saw Ma's eyebrows raise and she looked at me sideways.

"Why are we here?" She said, just as the man behind the counter asked how he could help us.

"Could we take a look at one of your BB guns?" I asked in my most mature voice. The man put the gun on the counter and started to tell us a little bit about it, "a BB gun is an air gun. It is designed to shoot metallic projectile balls called BB's."

As he spoke, with Ma standing behind me, he stopped and asked, "is this gun for you?"

"Well, it might be," I said.

He then proceeded to tell me how I'd have to go to the police station first and take a shooting test, and that I couldn't get a license until I did that.

I was upset, I hadn't realized that was a thing. I pulled Ma aside, "Ma, can you go to the police station and take the test for me so I can buy this BB gun?"

"Gary, *no*. I cannot. I do not want you to have this, and I'm not taking the test for you."

"But all of my buddies' moms did this for them," I lied. I didn't know anyone but Scott Windslow who had a BB gun, and he lived two streets over.

"I doubt that. Not to mention, what if you accidently shot a person? I'd be in trouble because it was registered in my name."

"BUT, MA!" I was annoyed at how selfish she was being and started to make a scene.

Ma stared at me with a look I wasn't used to getting, and said, "absolutely not. This discussion is closed."

We didn't speak the entire bus ride home, and I stormed off as soon as the doors opened.

That night, Ma and Dad gave me a card with $25.00 dollars in it and a nice cake.

It didn't take long for me to forget about the BB gun and move on to other things.

Years later, I found out that while the gun salesman told me about the BB gun, Ma stood behind me at the gun counter and shook her head, *no*, the entire time. He made the whole story up about having to go to the police station for a test.

Can you imagine someone standing behind your back and controlling a situation on your behalf without you knowing? *I mean, who does that!?!*

Clown!

I Call the Fat

In a house with three boys, two parents, and an aunt or two, food played a big role in my childhood. The one bathroom situation did too, but don't even get me started on that shit right now.

We had our staples when it came to food. Wednesday was Prince Spaghetti Day. Ma served pasta with a watery meat sauce. Friday was hot dogs, baked beans, and brown bread. On Saturday afternoons, radishes were always on the menu for Dad.

He'd get a big bag of radishes, cut off the ends, float them in a bowl of water, and get some salt. He'd sit there and eat them all while he watched the baseball game. He'd pierce them with his pen knife, throw some salt on them, and drink a six-pack of Schlitz.

The after effects of this routine where brutal. Between the farting and radish-smelling belches, we kids knew that the best thing to do was to get a game of Relievio started for a few hours outside while we waited for the house to air out.

73

Not that we minded being outside on a Saturday afternoon. That's when Mister Softee stopped by. We'd be in Ridley Field or playing stick ball in the street and we'd hear his carousal music jingle before we saw his truck.

Most of us knew to save a few quarters from our allowance to get an ice cream on Saturdays. For those who forgot, Mister Softee gave them a free piece of Bazooka Bubble Gum. He felt bad for them. He was a pretty good guy.

We loved all his ice cream, but nothing beat the Screwballs and the Vanilla-Fudge Swirl Push-Ups.

One time on my birthday, while I sat on the steps and Dad watered the grass, we heard Mister Softee's jingle down the street.

"Gary, want a banana split for your birthday?" Dad asked as he put down the hose.

"Would I ever!"

Mister Softee's banana splits were the best. They came in a blue, plastic banana boat and had two swirls of vanilla soft serve on each end and a swirl of chocolate soft serve in the center. They were topped with strawberry, pineapple, chocolate sauce, whipped cream, nuts, a sliced banana, and a cherry.

To this day, that was my favorite summer memory. Dad, in an effort to keep my brothers from calling *"no fair,"* bought them both small sundaes of their own. We all sat on my front steps eating that ice cream as fast as we could so it wouldn't melt. I still remember the ice cream headache!

One of my favorite fall memories, come to think of it, revolved around food too. It was cold out that day. After a long walk home from school, I stopped to look at our windows before going in. They were steamed up, and I knew that meant Ma had a steaming, hot bowl of either fish chowder or vegetable noodle soup waiting for me. I still get a warm, good feeling every time I see a steamed-up window when it's cold out.

While Saturday afternoon consisted of ice cream and radishes during the summer, Saturday nights were even better. We'd either have western omelets or deep-fried trout served on paper bags if Uncle Sammy came over.

We loved when Uncle Sammy came over. He was always tan from the work he did in construction, and his voice was as big as he was. The first thing he said (yelled) when he came in the door was, "I'M HERE WITH THE FISH! LET'S GET THIS SHOW ON THE ROAD!"

He emptied his brown paper bag and took out the fish wrapped in wax paper. He usually brought large trout with shinny scales and big gold eyes that he caught fishing that day. We'd sit and watch while Uncle Sammy and Dad gutted the fish on the back porch, their Schlitz never far from reach.

They chopped off the heads, which freaked Aaron out, but Mike and I thought it was cool. Then, they sliced the fish right down the center and give the blood a minute to pour out before they pulled out the guts. Next, they'd wash them and roll them in cornmeal and drop the fish into the pot of hot oil on the stove. The kitchen had a cloud of grease floating over the room like something out of those *National Geographic* photos of the smog in China.

Ma usually sat in the other room in her rocking chair, knitting and enjoying the break.

My brothers and I used to listen to the crap Dad and Uncle Sammy talked about.

"Dan, when was the last time you saw Shabootie?" Uncle Sammy would holler.

"I haven't seen that son-of-a-bitch in ages."

"Well, you won't see him ever again either. He's dead," he yelled. Then, he'd tell the big story of how Shabootie died, and we'd sit mesmerized.

Sometimes they wouldn't talk much and instead listen to the country oldies while they cooked. I grew up with knowing all the Country Greats. I liked to hear Hank Williams belt out over the 8-track player:

"Can you hear that lonesome whippoorwill?
He sounds too blue to fly.
The midnight train is whining low.
I'm so lonesome I could cry."

If it wasn't Hank Williams, it was Johnny Cash:

"I hear the train a comin'. It's rollin' 'round the bend,

And I ain't seen the sunshine, since, I don't know when.

I'm stuck in Folsom Prison, and time keeps draggin' on.

But that train keeps a-rollin' on down to San Antone."

I used to wish that I could have a beer with them and listen to the music without my brothers hanging around. Instead, I'd drink my Coca-Cola and pretend it was a beer.

After our bellies were full and after Uncle Sammy left, we'd go in with Dad and watch *S.W.A.T.* I didn't mind Saturday nights at all.

Every Sunday though, while the rest of us had Sunday dinner, which could be anything from American Chop Suey, stuffed peppers, or sausage with beans and creamed corn, my Dad got his reward for working his ass off at two jobs for the lot of us.

He'd get a good steak with sautéed mushrooms and spinach. None of us ever bitched about this for a couple of reasons. First, we were full and well-fed. Second, we all agreed with Ma when she said that he deserved it.

That didn't stop us from bitching though about who got the fat from Dad's steak. By fat, I mean the big hunk of fat that Dad trimmed off of his fried steak. It was pure rubber, but it was so juicy and we sucked on it like a cud. Ma hated that we did this.

The rule was that we couldn't call it until Ma served Dad his steak. For instance, we couldn't call it on Thursday. It was a tricky business because sometimes I'd forget about the fat until it was too late and one of my stupid brothers would yell, "*I call the fat!*"

Aaron was the biggest prick about it. When he'd get it, he'd shove it in his mouth and sit there smacking his lips, and he'd tell us that it was the best piece of fat so far.

This didn't go over well with the rest of us. One time, after one of his obnoxious displays, I took a fistful of pepper from the kitchen and when Dad wasn't looking; I blew it right into his face. He coughed and sneezed and the fat went flying right out his mouth and onto the floor. Our dog, Digger, ran over and gobbled it up in a nanosecond. Apparently, Digger wanted in on calling the fat too!

79

When Aaron started yelling, I sauntered out of the room with a small smile on my face. "I don't know what he's talking about" was my answer when dad asked what he was bitching about. But when Dad looked away, I balled up my fist and shook it in Aaron's direction. That shut him up.

Another thing that pissed me off about food was that every night one of the neighborhood kids would happen to stop by at dinnertime. It wasn't always the same neighbor, but whenever they'd come, Ma invited them in like it was no big deal. It pissed me off. Those pricks knew we were eating, and they just happened to conveniently stop by and act like they didn't know.

I bitched to Ma about it all the time. She'd just say, "you'll understand one day."

"Understand what? They're moochers, and they're treating you like a sucker!"

That was always Dad's que to tell me to shut up.

I understood why Ma did it a few months later. I went into Shawn's house. He was this little Irish kid from the tenement next door, and one of our frequent dinner guests.

We were getting a game together one afternoon and we stopped by his apartment so he could get his baseball glove. His dad was passed out on the sofa, a whiskey bottle on the end table, and a mess all around. There were clothes everywhere and the trash barrel was overflowing.

I remember thinking how my Old Man would drink, but never like that. It was two in the afternoon and in the middle of the week, for Christ's sake.

When Shawn came downstairs, his glove slipped out of his hand and it landed on the end table and knocked a glass to the floor.

His dad shot up into a sitting position on the couch and yelled, "what the *fuck* is going on? Keep the fucking racket down!"

"Sorry, Pops. Sorry about that," Shawn said, and we quickly backed out of the door.

As we made our way to the park I asked him where his Ma was. He said she left a few months ago and never came back. That now it was just him and his dad.

Later that night, Shawn stopped by at dinnertime to see if I could come out. It was the same old song and dance. Ma told him he caught us *right at dinnertime* so come in and join us. She said we could go out when we were done eating. He always said "are you sure it's ok" she always said "of course. She told him to wash up and grab a seat at the table. When Shawn came back to the table, Ma was asking Dad about his day at work while she prepared a plate for Shawn. She placed a stuffed pepper, a helping of corn, and some bread and butter on his plate, along with a big glass of milk, all while talking to Dad.

Shawn waited to eat while she proceeded to serve the rest of us. I looked at Ma, impressed at how she could stretch a meal and always had enough for our guests. I thought about all the mouths she's fed, and all the neighborhood kids who took their place at our table. Those "moochers" who didn't get a hot meal at home. Ma knew this and never made them feel ashamed about it.

I wondered if this was the first decent thing Shawn had eaten all day. I sat there awhile, looking at

Ma and thought, *she's a sucker alright! But it'd be nice if I grow up to be a sucker like that.*

A HALLOWEEN STORY

The coolest part of our house was the creepy-ass cellar. It had damp, stone walls and smelled like mothballs, mold, and what I imagined radon smelled like.

Cement held each stone together. Because of the age of the cellar, sometimes a chunk of cement fell out and the hole would turn into a great place to hide things. Many coins, love notes from girls, and pages from Dad's *Playboy* found their way into these hiding spots.

There was always a chill in the air down there and an overall creepy feeling. The washer and dryer were against the wall at the bottom of the stairs. Ma said she got the creeps every time she went down to do laundry. There was an old work bench with a few of Dad's tools on one side of the cellar and a big, leaky oil tank that our alley cat, Monday, always slept on top of on the other side.

The chimney was exposed in the center of the cellar and next to it was the oil burner. The little door to the boiler had fallen off so you could see the open pilot flame, which added to the spooky atmosphere.

I used to chase my brothers around the chimney many times when we were younger. I told them the cellar turned me into a monster and then I'd chase them. It usually made them cry.

At the far end of the cellar there was a door. The stone wall continued on the other side of the door, and there were old, wooden stairs that led up to the bulkhead and out to the backyard. No one liked to open that door. There was no light in the stairwell and it was scary as Hell if anyone decided to pull a trick and shut the door behind you.

The stairs that led to the cellar from inside the house were narrow and steep. My brother, Aaron, used to hide under them whenever there was a tornado warning in the summer. He packed a lunch, a flashlight, and his portable radio (tuned into local AM news). He'd sit and wait all day for a tornado that never came. He was a freak that way.

Just to be a dick and to mess with him, I'd yell down the stairs, "MY GOD! You wouldn't believe how black the sky is. We'll get it this time for sure!"

He'd flip out and tell me to get the rest of the family and take shelter. I'd just ignore him while he screamed like a lunatic. After a while, he'd calm down and come back upstairs.

The cellar was good for games like flashlight tag and séances. Later on, we figured out that it was also good for sneaking a girl down for a make out session when Ma was busy.

Once, I went down to get Ma's laundry basket and when I turned on the light, Michael jumped up from a blanket that was on the floor. Laurie Marshall, a girl from up the street, was sitting on the blanket.

I looked at them and didn't say anything. After squirming a bit, Mike yelled, "*what?*"

I smiled and said, "oh what have we got going on here?"

"Shut up, Gary. We were just talking," Mike said red in the face.

"Talking, oh really? Were ya, Mike—just talking? Is that what you were doing?" I knew I sounded like a total dick. "Looks like you were doing a hell of a lot more than just talking—*with the lights out!*"

"Why do you have to be such a dick? Go back upstairs," Mike said.

"Yeah, I'll go upstairs, but the lights are staying on. It's for your own good," I said imitating those stern parents you hear on TV.

Mike glared at me and said, "whatever—you're a dick."

"Hey Mike! Ridley Field. Shelly. *Remember*?"

I looked at Laurie, winked, and said, "see ya later, Laurie Marshall." Then, to Mike I said, "see ya later, dinkweed."

Everyone knows it's a big brother's job to bust a little brother's balls. That's life.

All of that stuff about the cellar was good but our haunted houses were the best part. I was raised in the *Creature Double Feature* days. Vampires, Frankenstein, Godzilla, Werewolves—I loved all the monsters. Three or four times a year my brothers and I would create a haunted house—it didn't matter what time of year it was. Each haunted house was more elaborate than the one before. And each had a story that one of us wrote to fit a theme we all agreed on.

Our supplies came from stuff lying around the house. We banged out sets using old wood and nails from Dad's stockpile. We painted backdrops to create a maze full of scary shit on Ma's old and tattered table cloths. We placed a few mirrors around the maze to make it seem bigger. Old Christmas string lights provided just enough light to see where we were going, but it still kept things scary.

There was money in this business. We'd gather a group of kids from the neighborhood and charge a dime to walk through the haunted house.

For all the effort we put into our haunted houses, the actual walk would only take about two minutes. And that's if we dragged it out. We loved scaring the shit out of the kids, and they must have liked it because they'd always show up with a dime.

We'd start the walk off in the backyard with one of the brothers (usually Michael since he was good at being very serious) reading the story. Mike would sit all the kids in a circle in the backyard and read it very dramatically.

When the story was finished, he'd line them up, collect their dimes, and head down the bulkhead. He would knock three times on the door to signal the rest of us. It was mostly me and Aaron running the haunted walk, but sometimes my cousin Billy helped out.

Mike would walk in while keeping everyone huddled together and shut the door behind them. It would be pitch black. After a long minute in the dark, he would flip on the Christmas lights and walk them through the maze.

We would then try our best to scare the living hell out of everyone. We would know we succeeded by a few benchmarks: Did Angie pee her pants? How loud was everyone screaming? Did anyone cry?

The end of the maze dropped everyone back at the entrance. There was usually a mad rush up the stairs of the bulkhead and out of our yard. The next few hours usually consisted of the group sitting on their neighbors' steps talking about our haunted walk and how scary it was.

My brothers and I took this as success and started planning the next one.

Because of our haunted houses, I already had a topic when Mrs. Early assigned us a five-page essay in October. I found myself looking forward to writing it even though Mrs. Early only gave us a week to do it. While everyone was whining about it in class, I started imagining what I'd write in my head. For the first time in my life, I couldn't wait to get home and get started on homework.

The following Monday, Mrs. Early didn't try to hide her surprise when I handed in my assignment. She looked down at the essay in her hands, then at me, then back at the essay, and then back at me.

"Gary, wow, I'm eager to read this," she said.

It would have been a waste of time for me to get pissed off at her. She had a point. I usually screwed off in class and barely bothered to come up with an excuse for late homework.

But this time was different. This time I was eager to have her read it. I'd have to wait until Friday to find out what she thought about it.

Our essays were the first thing she covered that day.

90

"Class, I finished reading your essays. The grammar was atrocious in a few of them. And not to single anyone out, but do we really think it's appropriate to write about the bodily functions of a dog? You know who you are, and I want to see you after class. That said, there were a few good stories, and one that really stood out."

I straightened up in my seat a bit.

"It was quite good and spooky, which is fitting since it's almost Halloween," she said. "There are one or two slightly inappropriate comments in this story, but I will overlook them." She paused and continued, "since it's almost Halloween, I thought it would be a nice treat to share this story with the class." She sat in her chair and began reading…

AN EYE FOR AN EYE

Mike was mad. He walked this path a hundred times. He swore he could do it with his eyes closed—where the heck did he go wrong?

It was a beautiful and sunny October day. The leaves had turned red, orange, and yellow and stood out vividly against a bright, blue sky. The air was cool and crisp. It was the kind of air that made his nose sting when he took a deep breath.

He lived on the edge of seventy-five acres of conservation land, and he decided that it was a great day to take a walk on the trails. He'd taken walks this way many times. He knew every twist and turn, every stream, and every tree.

So, how the heck did he end up in this situation?

He'd been out on the trails for three hours. Every time he tried another path, thinking it was the right one, he'd end up somewhere new. He was starting to get concerned. He hadn't prepared for a long hike—he was armed only with a thermos of water, a few sticks of gum, a pack of cigs, and a lighter.

He'd left his house after eating lunch at one o'clock. He planned to take an hour hike, come home, and then shower up for his date with Mags.

Maggie Horn worked at Prince Book Store in Nashua, and he'd been trying for two months to get her to agree to a date. He finally wore her down. He planned to pick her up, take her to the Grotto for some Italian, and then over to the movie theater to catch the new John Wayne movie. If he was lucky, he'd get the goodnight kiss he was hoping for, and maybe a goodnight feel, though he knew this was probably wishful thinking.

He didn't want to blow it. But now, it seemed like his date might not happen. It was already four o'clock and soon it would get dark.

He started thinking of what would happen if he had to sleep out in the woods. He was hungry, but knew he'd be okay if he had to go a night without food. The gum would help him when he felt hungry and keep his mouth moist. Water was the big thing, and he knew he'd have to conserve it. He was also glad he had decided against picking this week to quit smoking—his lighter would come in handy.

As the sun started to set and the temperature started to drop, he knew he needed to pick a spot to hunker down for the night and start a fire. He started collecting branches and leaves when he heard something behind him.

"What was that?" he yelled jumping back, "who's there?" He spun around and eyed the trees around him. In his peripheral vision he thought he saw a shadow move near a tree to his right.

"Okay, Mike," he said to himself out loud, "knock it off. You got a long night ahead of you." He took a deep breath and continued to collect kindling for a fire.

He dug out a circular area and arranged some wood and leaves to make a fire. He remembered from his Boy Scout days that it was best to light a fire in a clearing so the smoke rose above the trees if you were lost.

The only problem was that no one would be looking for him. His parents were gone for the weekend and wouldn't be home until Sunday night. Mags would think he chickened out and stood her up. His best hope was to wake up in the morning and spend the day finding his way out. He didn't want to let his mind imagine anything beyond tomorrow though.

When he got down on all fours to get the fire going, he felt something tickle the back of his neck. He jumped up and spun around again. He smacked at the back of his neck, and when he brought his hand down he noticed a spider on his hand.

"You *suck!*" he yelled as he flicked it to the ground and stepped on it. He knew this was going to be a rough night. He had no jacket, just a sweat shirt and little else to shield him from the bugs that would be sharing his bed tonight.

"Man up, Mike, you have to do this buddy," he told himself out loud.

He bent down to get the fire going again, but then he heard leaves crunch behind him. He turned quickly but no one was there. He told himself that it was the wind. He was imagining things now.

He figured the best thing to do was to take a piss and hit the sack. It made no sense to stay up and creep himself out. He just had to get to sleep and make it through the night.

95

He went to the tree line, unzipped his fly, and started to pee. While he was peeing, he heard the crunch again and this time swore he felt cold breath on the back of his neck. He jumped, getting pee on his leg and looked around. Just like the other times, no one was there. He was hyperventilating now and stopped to catch his breath.

He zipped up his fly and walked back to the fire. He found a log to lean against and laid there for about an hour looking at the stars. He hoped Mags would give him the chance to explain when he got out of here.

Finally, and mercifully, he fell asleep.

Late that night, as the fire burned out, Mike woke abruptly to something tickling the back of his neck and what felt like a cool breath of air on his neck again. He reached back as he yelled, "son-of-a-bitch!" Convinced that he would find another spider.

Only it was not a spider. As he reached back he grabbed what felt like bone. He turned onto his side, and in the glow of the dying fire, he saw he was staring into the face of a very old woman wearing a black cloak.

She hunched over him. She was missing teeth, had glowing, green eyes and a very long nose. Her boney hand clutched the back of Mike's neck. She stared at Mike, licked her lips, and said, "eyes, eyes, please. *Eyes.*"

Terrified, Mike tried to break free from her boney grasp but could not. She threw her head back and cackled loudly. Then, she pulled him closer to her face. He could smell her rancid breath.

She said in a wet voice, all laughter gone and enraged, "EYES, PLEASE! EYES, PLEASE! *EYYYYEEEESSSSS,* PLEASE!"

Two houses down from Mike's house, his neighbor, Mr. Homer, woke up to a scream coming from the woods behind his house. He got up and went out to his back deck and heard it again. It was a blood-curdling, terrified scream.

He ran back inside, grabbed his gun, and went back out to the deck to have a look. No one was there. He heard nothing. He saw nothing. He stood there for a few minutes and thought he must have been dreaming. Or maybe it was a fisher cat. He went back to bed.

Two days later, when he saw on the news that Mike's parents had reported him missing, he wondered if the scream had been a dream after all. He told the police what he had heard that night.

It took Sheriff Palmer and his crew two more days to find Mike's body. They found him in a clearing a mile from his home. His death was ruled as hypothermia due to overexposure.

It was strange to everyone that a kid so familiar with the woods could get lost so close to home. Even stranger though, was the condition of the body. Sheriff Palmer had only heard of something like this happening once, a few years back in these very woods. When the crew was done securing the area and bringing the body out, the Sheriff walked slowly behind them wondering what kind of an animal only ate the eyes and nothing else.

From the corner of his eye he thought he saw a black shadow move near the tree line, but it was gone when he turned to look.

"Best move on out quickly, boys," he hollered from the rear. "The sun is starting to go down."

The class was silent when Mrs. Early finished reading my story. She waited a moment then said, "that story was written by Gary Simpson. Nice job, Gary. It was very captivating and spooky."

A few of my friends from my neighborhood who were in class just sat looking at me. I couldn't tell if they were shocked I wrote it or if they liked it.

As we filed out of the room, Kyle caught up to me and said, "dude, that was creepy! Is any of it true?"

I saw my opportunity and said, "I don't wanna talk about it, but I'll see you next week for the haunted house."

When I got home I told Mike and Aaron, "Boys, we have our next theme!"

THE KING

I used to hang around with Robbie Decker. His family lived a few streets over. Robbie was a good kid, but kind of strange sometimes. Someone, my Grams would call, "eccentric."

He used to put duct tape on everything. If he ripped his pants, he'd put a piece of duct tape on the rip to hold it together. If you went in his bedroom he'd have silver tape holding everything up on his walls. He used it to hang posters, shelves, and even a few of his old stuffed animals from when he was younger. Yeah, he hung his old teddy bears on his bedroom walls with silver duct tape. Friggen weird. I asked him why one time, and he just shrugged and said, "why not? It works." He had a point I guess.

Robbie's strangeness was something he inherited from his both of his parents. They were nice people. They were always friendly and weren't yellers or constantly crabby like some of my other friends parents were. I didn't mind hanging out there with Robbie, his folks didn't hound us.

His dad had jet black hair that was slicked back with so much grease I'd be afraid to light a match around it. He used to wear these giant belt buckles with turquoise stones and big knuckle rings. He'd wear the rings and belt buckle all the time. He worked at the Waterworks and they made him wear a green uniform. The big belt and rings looked weird as shit with the uniform but he wore them anyway.

Robbie's mom was a flaming redhead. Like, a Lucy redhead. Only she used to wear a giant beehive hairdo. It was kind of alarming to look at. She was a meaty woman, but loved short, polyester dresses and shiny, white go-go boots.

Robbie had a sister a few years younger named Allison. She used to hang around with Angie and have her over the house to play with Barbies when I was there sometimes. Other than saying "hi," we never bothered much with them. Robbie and I would usually just stay in his room and listen to music.

Allison was actually pretty normal, and from what I could see, she wasn't strange like the rest of them. As a matter of fact, you could tell by looking at her that someday when her jugs came in, she'd probably be a pretty good-looking chick.

One time, something happened that would top every one of the odd things about the Decker's that I'd seen so far.

It was a hot summer evening, and the Decker's were one of the few families that had an air conditioner in their kitchen. This was rare in our neighborhood; most of my friends didn't have air conditioning at all. We only had one in my parents' bedroom, and we were lucky to have it. In the summer, my brothers and I would camp out on my parents' bedroom floor with our sleeping bags when it was a real hot night. But Robbie's family had two—one in his parents' room and one in the kitchen.

So I didn't mind hanging out there at all. This one time I went over after dinner to play Battleships with Robbie in his kitchen.

His mom gave us each a bottle of Coca-Cola and a bowl of chips and reminded us to keep it down because they were watching NBC *Nightly News* with David Brinkley. I remember thinking that I didn't give a shit what they were watching, but said, "okay, ma'am. We'll keep it down."

Robbie and I noshed on chips and gulped down our Cokes while we played Battleships. We called out codes, "B4, D8, A9, *CRAP*! You sunk my battleship!" Robbie kicked my ass the first two games, but that was o.k. we were playing best out of 5, I still had a shot.

All of the sudden, from the other room, we heard a sound that made us both jump. It was unlike anything I'd heard before. It sounded like someone being attacked by a bear or something. Like a wailing kind of sound that was mixed in with blood-curdling screams.

Robbie and I jumped to our feet. Not sure what to do, we stood there for a second, frozen. It was coming from the living room where Mr. and Mrs. Decker were. We were almost afraid to see what was going on.

As we made our way slowly to the doorway of the room, the first thing I noticed was that Mr. Decker was not in his big overstuffed easy chair and Mrs. Decker was not in her rocker. I looked down and saw them both cowering on the floor, they were hugging each other, rocking back and forth and sobbing.

Robbie yelled in panic, "MOM! DAD! WHAT'S WRONG?"

Then, Allison and Angie, who had been upstairs playing with Barbies, came running into the living room.

"WHAT? *What's going on*?" Allison yelled.

All four of us stood together watching the Decker parents in horror. Then, Mrs. Decker screamed, "ELVIS IS DEAD! *Oh Dear Lord! Sweet Baby Jesus!* ELVIS IS DEAD."

Then, Mr. Decker raised his hands and screamed, "leave the room, children. *LEAVE THE ROOM*!"

Robbie, with tears in his eyes, turned to me and said, "maybe you guys should go."

Allison just looked at her parents again, rolled her eyes and muttered, "*Jesus Christ*. I guess I'll talk to you tomorrow, Ang." She turned and walked back upstairs unfazed.

As we walked out the front door, we heard Mrs. Decker sobbing and yelling, "what'll we do, Chester? *What'll we do?*"

It also sounded like Robbie might have joined them in their lamenting.

Angie and I walked most of the way home in silence. We were both in shock. It wasn't that we didn't like Elvis, I mean, he was cool and all, but I don't think either of us had ever seen grown-ups act that way about anything.

The hair and the belt buckles Mr. Decker wore made sense to me now.

When we got to the end of our street, Angie started to walk faster than me, and I called to her, "Ang, slow down. Remember: Only fools rush in."

She looked at me for a minute then we both laughed. When we got to Angie's, I told her to have a good night.

She chuckled and said, "you too, Gary."

I remember thinking as I walked away, that it was a Tuesday and it was August 16, 1977.

So much for "long live the king." The king was dead.

R.I.P. Elvis.

LET'S DANCE

Susan and Arnold Silva lived at the top of the street. Susan was one of Ma's friends, and when they got together, I'd hang out with her son, Mitch.

He was a chubby kid with glasses and had a pretty good sense of humor. He wasn't really into girls like I was, but he was into James Bond and got a cool spy kit for his birthday so I didn't mind hanging out.

We'd spend most of our time screwing around with the spy kit. Our parents confiscated the x-ray glasses after we lied and told the girls in the neighborhood we could see their vaginas. The whole fucking place was up in arms!

We put the kit to good use one Saturday night at a party the Silva's hosted for their grown-up friends. Mrs. Silva invited me to sleep over in the hopes that I would keep Mitch out of her hair. Ma had my grandma come over to babysit my two brothers so her and Dad could go.

I thought the party was kinda stupid to be honest. The women all wore long maxi dresses and the guys wore leisure suits. It looked like they were going to a fucking prom for *cripe's sake*. In reality, they were just in someone's living room. Whatever turns you on, I guess.

I didn't want to wait for my parents to get ready, so I went to the Silva's early. When I got there, Mrs. Silva gave us some snacks and two tray tables, and told us to go in Mitch's room and play and keep away from the party.

"No monkey business, boys," his dad said as we walked down the hall.

"Yes, sir," we replied in unison. So, of course, as soon as we got inside of Mitch's bedroom we came up with a plan.

We knew that the party would take place mostly in the living room. We saw his mom setting up wine, Scotch glasses, and records there.

The dining room was next to the living room and was separated by French doors that had curtains on them. In the dining room was another door that led into the hallway. We planned to stakeout a corner on either side of the French doors after the party started,

107

and then we'd peek through the curtains and watch it all unfold.

Mitch snuck into the living room when Mr. and Mrs. Silva were in the kitchen preparing snacks. I was the lookout. Mitch left two little receivers from the spy kit behind a chair on either side of the French doors. The receivers had little hollow centered cords with an ear piece attached to the ends. He ran the cords close to the wall under the doors so that we could use the ear pieces to listen to what was going on. It was some cool shit.

We wanted to see what they talked about when no kids were around and how they acted when they got tipsy. We hoped to see a fight or at least a lampshade on someone's head!

We waited patiently for everyone to arrive. Around eight o'clock, people started showing up. Ma and Dad were the first guests.

"Hello Carole and Danny! And *yay*—you brought Marie and Ronnie," Mrs. Silva hollered. Less than five minutes later we heard them greet another couple. Again, Mrs. Silva hollered, "oh good, that's all of us. Let's get this party started!"

108

The third couple was Teresa and Roland Cooper. They lived at the bottom of our street. I didn't know them well because their kids were young so they weren't allowed to play outside of their yard. They seemed to be friendlier with Mr. and Mrs. Silva.

"What can I get everyone to drink?" Mr. Silva asked.

The guys all wanted Scotch on the rocks and the ladies wanted wine. Me and Mitch figured we'd let the drinks flow a bit before we hid in the next room. After about half an hour we took our spots.

The guys were on one side of the room talking about work and the shitty game the Boston Patriots played the other night.

"I lost *ten-fucking-bucks* on that game," Dad said.

"Motherfuckers! I lost twenty! Don't tell Marie," Uncle Ronnie said as he lit a cigarette and mixed some Pepsi in his Scotch.

The guys were swearing more than I was used to hearing, but the women weren't paying attention. They were across the room talking about how funny Carole Burnet was and how handsome Lyle Wagner

109

was. They gossiped about some lady at the church who supposedly sat in the front pew and flashed her underpants at the young priest on the alter.

"*God*, forgive her," Auntie Marie said, "you could go to Hell for doing that."

After about half an hour, we were starting to get bored when Mr. Silva stood up and said, "okay, ladies come over here. Let's put on some records and dance. We'll start with a slow one to warm us up!"

As Elvis began to croon, "are you lonesome tonight, are you lonesome tonight, are you sorry we drifted apart...," Mr. Silva walked up to Mrs. Silva and put his hand out and said, "shall we?"

Mrs. Silva stood up and said, "certainly."

Next, Ma walked over to Dad and said, "come on, Danny. Let's not let them have all the fun!"

Dad stood up and said, "sure, why the hell not?"

Soon everyone was dancing.

After a couple of slow songs, and with a few more drinks, things started to get interesting. Mr. Silva changed records and put on "The Twist" by Chubby Checker. Ma jumped up and started twisting away, she was pretty good too! Soon every couple started twisting.

You could tell they were all pretty toasted at this point. After "The Twist," some jitterbug thing came on.

Mr. Silva turned to Ma and said, "Carole, let's show them how it's done!"

Before Ma could answer he grabbed her and they started to jitterbug. Mrs. Silva grabbed Uncle Ronnie by the hand and they started to dance. Then, Mr. Cooper grabbed Aunt Marie. Before Mrs. Cooper had a chance to grab Dad, he poured himself another Scotch on the rocks. He didn't seem to want to jitterbug. He looked like he'd rather watch than dance.

After that song finished, the music went into a slow song. "Unforgettable" by Nat "King" Cole. All the couples already on the floor continued to dance with one another. Dad looked relieved that Mrs. Cooper had excused herself to go to the restroom so he wouldn't have to ask her to dance. He sipped his Scotch and sat taking it all in.

I was behind the door, looking at his face, when I noticed he was scowling. He was staring straight ahead towards Aunt Marie. His eyebrows came together. I didn't know what was going on until I saw Mr. Cooper turn Aunt Marie in our direction. That's when Mitch and I noticed Mr. Cooper's right hand on Aunt Marie's ass! He had a handful of cheek and was giving it a good squeeze. Uncle Ronnie didn't seem to notice at all. Dad sat there staring and I could see that he was pissed.

When the song ended, "Chances Are" by Johnny Mathis came on. Dad jumped up and walked over to Mr. Silva and said, "I'm gonna cut in here. This is me and my girl's favorite song." Then, without missing a beat he said, "Ronnie, you should switch partners. Don't you and Marie like this one?"

Uncle Ronnie shook his head and said, "no this one isn't our song. I'll switch after this one."

"Dumbass," Mitch mouthed to me.

Dad looked annoyed, and as the dance started, Mrs. Cooper came back from the restroom and Mr. Silva grabbed her. "I'm without a partner and I'm looking for one!"

While they all danced, I saw Dad eye Mr. Cooper who was still grabbing Aunt Marie's ass. Dad was dancing next to Uncle Ronnie, so this time he nudged him and pointed to Aunt Marie. Uncle Ronnie looked, but he didn't say a word. He just kind of shrugged and blew it off.

Dad looked seriously pissed now. Aunt Marie, although a little red in the face, didn't seem to know what to do.

When the song ended, Dad yelled, "let's put a fast one on!"

Dad leaned close to Ma and said, "Carole, go sit with Marie." Ma got Aunt Marie and they walked back towards the chairs while Uncle Ronnie, Mrs. Silva, and Mrs. Cooper kept dancing.

Dad said, "hey, Arnold, would you mind getting a little more ice and some pretzels or something?"

Mr. Silva, always the good host, said, "Suzie, give me a hand in the kitchen, would ya?"

Mrs. Silva stopped dancing and went to the kitchen to help. Uncle Ronnie and Mrs. Cooper continued to dance. All the bases were covered. Mr. Cooper had a drink in his hand and was standing in front of the French doors Mitch and I were hiding behind. Dad walked across the room to Mr. Cooper and stood in front of him with his back to the dancers and everyone on the other side of the room. In a quiet voice, he said, "it looked like you were having a good time dancing with Marie."

Mr. Cooper smiled a drunken smile and said with a quiet chuckle, "you bet I did."

Dad reached across and took Mr. Coopers pointer finger and bent it in and Mr. Cooper flinched and started to sweat. I knew exactly what he was feeling because Ricky Pinchetta did it to me once for kissing his girl behind the school. It hurts like a bastard.

Mitch and I held our breath from the other side of the door. Dad got closer as he squeezed harder and said to Mr. Cooper, "you're gonna get your things and go before this gets even messier."

Mr. Cooper looked at him and nodded. Dad let go and went back to sit with the ladies. The song ended as the Silva's returned with pretzels and ice. The Coopers already had their jackets on and Mrs.

Cooper said, "I'm sorry to leave so abruptly but Roland is suddenly feeling under the weather."

"I'll bet he is," I thought.

As the four of them made their way into the hallway to say their goodbyes, Dad turned to Uncle Ronnie, shook his head and said, "no balls, Ronnie. Ya got no balls."

Ronnie shrugged and said, "why do I need 'em, Danny-Boy. I have you!"

Dad started laughing and said, "let's all have another dance!"

And just like that they all started dancing again. The atmosphere seemed lighter without the Coopers. The party lasted another hour with them dancing until the end.

As everyone wrapped things up, Mitch and I snuck back to his room.

As we laid in his bunkbeds listening to everyone saying goodbye, Mitch said to me in the dark, "wow, man. Your dad is a *badass*!"

He couldn't see my smile in the darkness as I said, "yeah, he is!"

BOOM!

One Friday evening, Ma asked me to walk down to the 24-hour store for a loaf of bread. It was only a few blocks away. I didn't bitch about it because I knew I'd probably run into some of my buddies on my way to the store.

About halfway there I saw Angie walking back. She was eating an ice cream sandwich and said, "hey Gar, how ya doing?" I told her I was good as we passed each other.

When I got to the store I grabbed the bread, and as I made my way out of the store, I ran into Mitch. We started talking about Mrs. Van Winkle who owned the store. She had no teeth, a mess of gray hair, and a phlegmy cough. She was kind of scary— all four feet nine inches of her. She kept a can of soup behind the counter, and she'd chuck it at anyone she saw trying to steal while yelling, "put it back! Get outta here, you *son-of-a-bitch*!" Usually it would end there.

Mitch told me that he almost took a can to the head after trying to pocket a Hershey bar. She missed and he laughed, so she ran out from behind the counter and pinched him in the leg and said, "GET YOUR ASS DOWN THOSE STAIRS AND BRING ME UP A CRATE OF APPLES!" She pointed to the cellar where she kept all her stock.

He said he did what she asked because he was afraid she'd call his dad. But then, the cellar lights went out while he was down there. In the dark, he heard heavy breathing from right next to him. Then, Mrs. Van Winkle said in a low voice, "you gonna steal from me again boy?"

Terrified, he said, "no ma'am. I promise."

Then she said in a low, creepy voice, "you better not, or I'll bury you under the floor down here and no one will ever find you."

She then reached out and pinched his butt cheek so hard he had a bruise that lasted a week. He stood frozen as he heard her walking up the stairs and then the lights switched back on. He grabbed the crate of apples and ran up the stairs. He put them on the floor on the side of the counter and turned to leave. He snuck a look back as he walked through the door, and she gave him a big, toothless grin.

"She's a fucking witch. I tell ya, Gary. Honest to God. She scared the shit outta me—she's an evil, scary, short witch!"

After his story, I was tempted to go back to steal something to see what would happen, but I thought better of it. I walked with Mitch down Main Street and said good night when we got to his house.

No one could predict what was about to happen next. To this day, I'll always regret stopping to talk to Mitch because maybe if I hadn't, I could have caught up with Angie and walked home with her. Maybe it would have changed everything. Then again, maybe not.

The house at the top of my street had a little shed on the side that bumped out and made an alcove. It blocked anyone below it from view, but anyone turning the corner could look right into the alcove. As I turned the corner I stopped for a second to register what it was I was seeing.

It was Jeremy Leroy, a kid who lived a few streets over. He was a big, ogre of a kid, and he looked creepy and dumpy. I didn't like him—never did—there was something *off* about him. He had his back to me and was struggling with something. As I made my way behind him, I saw he had one hand over Angie's mouth, and the other was trying to make its way done the front of her pants. She was squirming and moving with a look of complete and utter terror in her eyes. He had her pinned to the wall and was trying to get to her.

Dropping the bread, I walked up quietly behind Jeremy and grabbed him as hard as I could by the back of his neck. He stopped what he was doing, and I yelled, "ANGIE, RUN HOME NOW!" She got out of his grasp and ran down the street and into her house without looking back.

I turned Jeremy around and *BOOM*, the first punch I threw landed right in the bread box. He fell to his knees into the middle of the street. The second punch was right to the face and he fell on his side. I rolled him on his back and straddled him and started to levy a barrage of steady connects—one after the

119

other—to his face. He was bleeding and crying and begging me to stop. I couldn't because I couldn't get the look of terror Angie had in her eyes out of my mind. I was enjoying every punch.

After what seemed like a full five minutes of punches, I felt a hand on my shoulder, "ease up now, Gar, ease up!"

It was Frank from next door. "Come on now, buddy. You've done enough damage." I looked at Frank. He was in his boxers and had his after-dinner butt dangling in one hand. I knew he had been watching the whole thing from his porch. He helped me to my feet.

Jeremy ran away while I was distracted, and I yelled after him, "WE BETTER NEVER SEE YOUR FACE AROUND HERE AGAIN!" I heard him crying as he ran down the street.

Frank told me to sit with him on his front porch. He gave me a shot of whiskey from a bottle and my first cigarette. He told me I earned it and that he had a new-found respect for me. "You're still a dinkweed, kid. But now you're kinda the King of the

Dinkweeds—so that's cool." I left after I calmed down and finished the cigarette.

I hopped in the shower when I got home with my thoughts racing. What if I hadn't got there in time? The water felt good on my knuckles, and it helped clear my head. After thirty minutes of quiet, I dried off and put on my sweats.

When I walked out of the bathroom, I saw Mr. Martin standing in the living room with my parents. Ma walked over to me and said, "Gary, are you okay?"

Mr. Martin walked over and said, "son, I want to thank you for what you did for Angie. I don't want to think of what could have happened to her if you hadn't come by."

I just looked at him. I didn't know what to say. I didn't know if Dad was gonna be mad at me for beating the tar out of Jeremy. I hadn't planned on telling him.

Mr. Martin continued, "I went to pay Jeremy's dad a little visit, and we won't be hearing from them again. His dad is sending him to live with his aunt—

said the boy has been a problem for a while now." He said that last part to my parents.

He turned his gaze back to me and said, "anyway, son, thanks again." He shook my hand, then my dad's and said, "Danny, you have a great kid here." Then, he walked out the door.

I stood frozen in the living room not knowing what to say when Ma said, "let me see your hands. Your knuckles are all swollen. Let's get you some ice."

While she was in the kitchen, Dad looked me up and down for a minute, and then he put his hand on the top of my head and rustled up my hair. "You done good kid, you done good," he said.

He sat back in his chair and yelled, "hey, Carole, wanna grab me a beer while you're out there?"

I sat in the chair next to him and we watched *Star Trek* together as I iced my hand. Just as Captain Kirk was invited along with Spock to a parley aboard the Romulan flagship, I heard a knock on the back door. Ma had gone upstairs to change for bed, and Dad wasn't about to get up, so I answered the door.

I found Mary standing on the porch in the dark. The only light was the one shining out from the kitchen and the glow from the moon. "Why are you coming to the back door—what's up?"

Mary motioned for me to come out. I followed her and realized that she was crying.

"What's the matter—what are you crying for?" She looked at me and opened her mouth to say something, and then closed it.

With tears streaming down her cheeks, she moved closer into me, put her arms around my shoulders, and kissed me. It wasn't an open mouth kiss, but it was a long, soft, sweet kiss. I waited for her to pull away. When she did, she looked up at me and said, "you are a hero, Gary. Thank you for what you did for Angie." Then she gave me a final small kiss and ran off the porch before I could say a word.

I stood on the back porch and looked up at the stars for a while. They were bright tonight. The moon was full. I mulled over the kiss, and thought about everything that happened the past few hours. I thought of Mary, Angie, and Captain Kirk. I decided

123

that this hero stuff is pretty cool. I could get used to it.

ST. LOUIS

After Christmas, my brothers and I started
talking about the St. Louis Carnival that took place
every year in May. We'd plan to start saving our
allowance, but in the end, Michael was the only one
who ever did. Come carnival time, we usually
resorted to asking him for a loan, that he happily gave
us—with interest. It didn't matter to us though.
Nothing could stop us from going to that carnival.

The week leading up to the carnival, Michael and
I walked the long way home from school so we could
watch them assemble the rides. The Octopus was one
of the cool rides. It looked like a giant octopus. At the
center was a picture of an octopus and branching out
were giant, black tentacles that held the shiny, green
seats.

One afternoon, I caught the carny glancing over
at us as we watched them build. He was a greasy
looking guy with wild hair and he wore a pair of
jeans and a dirty t-shirt that said, "honk if you're
horny."

He called out to us, "wanna try her out, boys?"

We jumped at the chance to take the ride for a test spin. We got the same offer for the rest of the week, and so we got to try out all the rides before the carnival officially opened. Mac, the greasy carny, told us that we better not open our yaps and tell any of our friends because they'd all be wanting in on the deal.

We gave him our word, and mostly stuck to it.

Aaron was the only person who found out. He heard me and Mike talking about it in our room one night when we thought the little shit was asleep. He didn't walk home with us because he was still in elementary school and too little to make the walk home.

He was beyond pissed. He spent the first two days bawling and yelling at us. The last few days though, he swallowed his pride and asked us to tell him all about the rides.

He wanted to know about the scariest rides and which ones were worth the money. We told him the octopus was a definite go. The Scrambler, too.

We told him we weren't crazy about the Ferris Wheel. The builder told us, after we got stuck at the top twice that they "still needed to work out some bugs on this one." I remember that Michael said to me, as we were swinging back and forth at the very top, "I'm not coming on again. Why tempt fate?" It was something Ma would've said, but I knew what he meant.

The remaining carnies and staff showed up the day before the grand opening of the carnival. They set up the food booths and the game booths (which were a major rip-off).

Trixie was in charge of the fried dough booth. When I looked at Trixie, she looked like someone my Uncle Sam would have said was "ridden hard and put away wet." I was never quite sure what he meant, but I guessed it meant that she looked like she's seen better days.

Trixie had some miles on her. She had long, stringy hair, bad skin, and she didn't wear a bra. Her boobs were the first thing anyone noticed about her. She was about forty-years-old, so it kinda grossed me out that my eyes wandered there.

Her niece, Michelle, worked with her, but she wasn't anything like her aunt.

Michelle was about eighteen and very pretty. She had long brown hair and big blue eyes. Unlike her aunt, she wore a bra. I knew right off the bat that I'd be eating a lot of fried dough at this year's carnival.

That Saturday morning, Ma made us all eat breakfast because she knew we'd be loading up on crap for the rest of the day. After securing our loans with Michael, we walked down to the carnival where we planned to spend the whole day.

Six other guys from the neighborhood joined us. We talked all the way there about what ride we'd go on first. We all agreed on The Octopus. We waited in line together for it.

Once it was our turn, Mike and I sat down and stuck Aaron in between us. Ma swore that if we didn't keep an eye on him, we wouldn't go to the carnival again. We didn't want to risk it.

A few of the carneys recognized us from our test rides, and Mike and I felt kinda cool giving them high-fives. It looked like we had an in! A few of them even let Mike and I get on a couple of rides without taking our tickets. It pissed Aaron off even more!

As the day wound down, I went for my third piece of fried dough. I was trying to build up the guts to ask Michelle if she wanted to go on a ride with me. As I approached the truck, I noticed there was a guy working with her. I ordered another powdered sugar and cinnamon piece when Michelle said, "oh Gary! Hi! Geez, you sure do like this stuff, huh?"

"Sure do—can't get enough of it," I said.

Before I had a chance to deliver my next line asking when her aunt would let her take a break, Michelle said, "Gary, this is my boyfriend, Kevin."

I looked Kevin over. He had on a gray and red letter jacket and his hair looked like a Ken doll. I didn't like Kevin.

"Hey, Gary! How ya doin', man?" he asked.

"Good," I grunted, "see ya around, Michelle." And I walked away. No more fried dough for me.

I found my crew and we decided that the haunted castle was a good ride to end the night on. If I was being honest, I was ready to call it a night then and there. I had a hair across my ass about Michelle.

We all lined up and paired off. I put Mike and Aaron together, and I'd follow them as the odd man out.

Mary and Angie got in line behind us.

"Hi, guys! Have you been on this yet?" Mary asked.

"Nope," I said.

"Oh us too. Angie is scared," she responded.

We waited in line quietly until it was time to get on. I heard Angie yell, "*NOPE. I'M NOT GOING*," at the last minute. I turned around and saw her jump out of line.

"Come on, are you kidding?" barked Mary.

"Mary, come with me. Ang, stay right here and don't move until we get off," I said. With that Mary jumped in my cart, just as the bar lowered on our laps.

We made our way through the haunted house jumping at the creaking noises, cackling witches, and floating candelabras. A big animatronic clown popped out as we rounded the first corner. Mary grabbed my arm and clung tightly to me. She stayed that way as we turned the next corner and a skeleton

130

floated over our cart. She screamed and I laughed. And our eyes met.

I don't remember who moved in first, but we were kissing before I knew what happened. Not a quick kiss either. This time it was a long, French kiss. I wasn't sure how long it went on for, but she squeezed the back of my neck and I got a boner.

We only stopped because we were startled by the cart slamming through the doors and a spooky Dracula voice saying "I HOPE YOUR ENJOYED YOUR RIDE, AH HA HA" at the exit of the haunted house. We jumped apart. As our cart came to a halt, Mary hopped out and ran off to meet Angie.

I got off the ride and passed her while I looked for my bothers. She looked at me and was a little red in the face as she said, "see you later, Gary."

I stood there watching her walk away and it was a very long time before I thought of Michelle again.

Funny how things happen like that.

MICK

One summer afternoon, Frank came out of his house (a hand in the waistband of his boxers and a cigarette in his mouth) and stood on his back porch. I was sitting on my own porch—bored out of my mind.

Without even looking at me, he called over, "hey, dinkweed! I gotta go pick up my *fucking* cousin, Mick, again. Wanna come along for the ride?"

Having nothing better to do, I said, "Sure, just let me tell Ma."

"Yeah, well, hurry up!" he said as he flicked his butt. "I'll meet ya out front. I gotta put on some pants."

As we walked to his car, I saw Mary sitting on her steps.

"Don't go anywhere," he said, "I'll be right back." He walked over to Mary. I watched them talk for a minute, and then she went into her house. Frank stood at the fence, waiting. When Mary came out, she handed him a bag with flowers printed on it, and said, "please, don't forget to give it back."

132

"I won't. Thanks, Mary," he said as he walked back to the car.

"Get in, dinkweed, let's go get that pain-in-the-ass."

Mick was as ugly as a bucket of shit left out in the sun and he had a drinking problem. Every time he got shitfaced and belligerent, his buddies would leave him and he'd call Frank to pick him up.

Frank told me that a few months ago, while he was on his way out the door to pick up his friend, Dennis, the phone rang. It was Mick looking for a ride. He told him he'd pick him up on the way to Dennis' house.

Mick was shitfaced as usual when he climbed in Frank's car that time. The first thing he said to Frank was, "hey, listen. I know Dennis talks shit about me." The truth was that a lot of people talked shit about Mick—there was a lot of shit to talk about. He went on, "So, here's what we're gonna do. I'm gonna hide out in your trunk so that I can hear what that prick says about me. Don't tell him I'm there—don't even mention my name."

Frank liked that idea. It meant that he wouldn't have to listen to Mick's drunken rambles. He pulled over, helped Mick into the trunk, and went to pick up Dennis.

Dennis was waiting outside when he pulled up, and they spent the next five hours driving around hitting up the bars.

As they drove back to Dennis' house at the end of the night, Frank burst out laughing. He told him about Mick being in the trunk for the whole night. Dennis perked up and said, "dude, how could you not tell me? What if he's dead back there?"

"Maybe we should check on him," Frank said as he pulled the car over.

They both got out of the car and opened the trunk. They found Mick curled up in a smelly, wool blanket. He was sleeping like a baby.

Frank and Dennis laughed and got back in the car to bring Mick home.

Frank shook Mick hard to wake him up. He groaned and sat up. "What did he say about me?"

"Dennis decided he was staying in tonight, so I just drove you home."

"Oh okay. Okay. We'll get him next time, right?" he said as he crawled out of the trunk not even noticing Dennis in the passenger seat.

Yeah, next time you friggin' clown, Frank thought.

So once again, it fell on Frank to pick up Mick. Frank lit a butt and said, "this shit is getting old. I'm gonna teach that son-of-a-bitch a lesson. Been thinking about it for weeks."

I asked him what he meant, but he shook his head and said, "never mind. Just follow my lead."

We drove in silence the rest of the way. As we pulled into the parking lot of the Knickerbocker Club, we saw Mick dozing on a bench out front. Frank pulled up and yelled, "MICK!"

Mick woke up with a start and said, "took ya long enough, asshole."

"Motherfucker," I heard Frank say under his breath. "Yeah, yeah. Get in the back," he yelled.

Mick made his way to the car on wobbly legs, opened the back door, and dropped in. He was snoring a few minutes later. We drove aimlessly for

135

about fifteen minutes to make sure Mick was in a deep, drunken sleep.

Then, Frank pulled into a parking lot. He picked a spot secluded and far away from the other cars. "Dinkweed, hop in the back and give me a hand. I need you to hold his head steady so he doesn't move."

Frank shut off the car, and we both hopped into the back. I held Mick's head between my legs and put a hand on each side of his head. While I was positioning myself, I saw Frank open up the floral bag that Mary gave him. I smiled when I realized what Frank had planned.

"What's so funny? This prick has it coming," Frank whispered.

I just sat there quietly as Frank went to work. First, he spread pancake makeup on Mick's face until his face was completely beige and white. Next, using the black eye brow pencil he drew big, thick black eyebrows over Mick's. Then, he applied some sky-blue eye shadow and mascara. He finished with a lot of rouge and some ruby-red lipstick.

It dawned on me during this process that I knew more about makeup than I probably should have. In my defense, I'd seen Ma put the stuff on for years. She never put on as much as this though. I mean by the time Frank was done, Mick looked like that character Carol Burnett did, Nora, something or other.

Anyway, it was bad. But it was only the beginning.

When he was done, Frank told me to hop back in the front, and we started to drive around again. After fifteen minutes, he yelled back to Mick, "HEY, MICK! Wake up, man!"

It took Mick a few minutes to wake up. "Huh, what? What's up?"

"Hey, we're hungry. Let's go get something to eat. Where's that place you like again? The restaurant with that chick, the one you're too chicken to ask out."

Mick perked up. "Oh Mabel's," he said clearing his throat. "They have good meatloaf. Let's go there. Maybe Sherry's working."

"Oh yeah, Sherry. That's her name. Well, maybe you will get lucky, buddy," Frank replied.

We pulled into Mabel's ten minutes later. The sun was starting to set.

The host looked at us strangely as we walked in. "Hey, is Sherry on tonight?" Frank asked.

"Yes," said the host.

"Great, can we get a table in her section?" The host said it wouldn't be a problem.

Before Sherry made her way to our table, Frank leaned over and said, "Mick, chicks dig funny guys. Tell her a joke right out of the gate and be funny."

As soon as Sherry approached, Mick said, "hey, Sherry! How's it going, how are they hanging?"

Sherry took one look at Mick and started to laugh. She quickly caught on that Mick had no idea what he looked like. She laughed throughout the meal. She laughed every time Mick opened his mouth to tell a terrible joke. But she laughed hardest when he said, "hey, Sherry, can I take ya out sometime?"

Needless to say, Mick was in a pissy mood as we left the restaurant. "I pulled out all my best jokes. I mean I had her eating right outta my hand! I was on fire—you guys saw her laughing, but she didn't answer if I could take her out or not." He was feeling down. "You don't think it's me or something, do ya guys?"

"Nah, who knows, buddy. Sometimes there's no accountin' for taste," said Frank. He pulled the car over in front of Mick's house.

He yelled out as Mick walked inside, "hey, Mick! You fucking asshole. Take a look in the mirror when you get inside."

Mick turned around with angry painted eyebrows and smudged red lips and said, "ya know, Frank, you ain't no day at the beach to look at either. So, fuck off!"

We both started cracking up as we drove away, and I said, "I wonder if he'll ever call you for a ride again after he gets a look in the mirror?"

I found out later that Mick never called Frank for a ride after that. I may be an asshole, but Frank is the *king*!

GRAMPS

Every Sunday morning, my folks forced us all to go to the 8:30 mass with them at St. Michael's Parish. My parents would sit in the pew behind us. Ma said it was because Dad said we'd be too crowded in one pew, but I knew that was bullshit. Dad liked to sit behind us so he could swat us on the back of the head when we acted up. It happened every week.

After mass, we'd all get twenty-five cents to go to the corner store to get snacks. Then, Dad would take us for a ride through the country (by "country" I mean his old neighborhood in Dracut).

We drove the backroads, lined with trees, and listened to "Rambling Man" on the radio. I remember we sat on the side arm rest of the doors with the wind blowing in our hair. I don't remember if the car was equipped with seat belts, but I know we didn't wear them. It was freedom.

After our car ride, he'd take us home and make a big Sunday breakfast of bacon, eggs, beans, and pan-fried potatoes. This was our "family time," and it was *not* up for debate. I didn't mind though.

When breakfast was finished, Dad would make me go up to my grandparents' house and help out with anything they needed. Usually my grandmother would be out visiting friends or volunteering somewhere, and so most of the time it was just me and Gramps. I didn't mind visiting him because he'd let me make my weekly wish.

Gramps had a small Buddha statue that used to sit on his T.V., and he'd tell me to rub the Buddha's belly and make a wish. It was supposed to be good luck, I guess. He'd tell me to make a wish, "but don't make it stupid." It would be a stupid wish to ask for a million bucks because the Buddha didn't care about money. So, every week I closed my eyes, rubbed Buddha's belly and laid down my wish. I looked forward to that weekly wish.

I also liked visiting Gramps because he was always doing something different. One Sunday, as soon as I walked into the house, he said, "grab a bottle of Coke and come down the cellar with me."

I grabbed a cold Coke and followed him down. For some reason he used a flashlight instead of turning the lights on. At the bottom of the stairs, he took a sharp left and walked to a black curtain he had hung under the stairs. He motioned for me to step inside the little room he created. When we were both inside, he closed the curtain and shut off the flash light. He pulled a cord and the room was illuminated by the blue light he had in the light socket. The room was lined in black felt. He had glow in the dark stars everywhere. There was a picture of the moon on one wall and a picture of JFK on the other.

"I made a space capsule," he said. "What do you think?" He was always doing neat stuff like that.

Gramps was a cool son-of-a-gun. He used to wear vests and fedoras with blue jeans and loafers, and he always looked sharp. Once at a wedding, he had a lavender shirt, white pants, a big white and silver Elvis belt buckle, and shiny white shoes. If anyone else wore that, they'd look like a moron, but Gramps pulled it off. He had character, as Ma used to say.

I saw pictures of him when he was younger, and he was a good-looking guy. So were all his brothers. They were all tall, with dark hair, lean builds, and blue eyes. I hear all the ladies liked him. He used to tell me he had to "beat 'em off with a stick!"

That's why I wasn't surprised the day he told me the story about the paper shoes. The year was 1929 and Gramps was seventeen. He and his sixteen-year-old brother, Huck, decided they wanted to take a few girls out for a night on the town. They needed a few bucks to do this though and went to talk to their dad about it.

Great-Grampy Elmer owned a little food market. He had a pretty good business. He told them they'd make a deal. Since they both needed new shoes, he was going to give them each two dollars to get them, and he'd throw in an extra buck each if they'd help him out at the store that week. It was the week of Thanksgiving and he was busy.

Gramps said they both hopped right on that deal, and that Great-Grampy Elmer put them to work sweeping, restocking, loading, and unloading. All the hard work was worth it though when, at the end of the week, he handed them both their two dollars for shoes and an extra dollar for their dates. As they walked out the store he called after them, "don't forget: I want to see shoes with that money!"

"Sure thing, Pop," they responded.

As they walked up the street and over the bridge to buy shoes, Gramps had an idea. Mr. McGovern owned the funeral parlor down the street, and Gramps was friends with his son, Donnie. He told Huck they were taking a little walk to visit Donnie. Back in the day, funeral parlors used to have paper shoes for the corpses. They looked like real shoes only they were made out of cardboard.

Donnie opened the door and Gramps said, "hey, Donnie, we have a little proposition for you. Ya know those paper shoes your dad has for the dead guys? How much do those cost?"

Donnie looked thoughtfully at Gramps and said, "I don't know he doesn't sell them like that. They come with the casket."

"How 'bout selling me and Huck a pair—we'll both give you twenty cents."

Donnie stood there studying them for a few minutes and said, "make it twenty-five each and you got a deal."

After the money was exchanged, Donnie had them wait at the corner. He said his dad would have his hide if he caught him taking the shoes.

Half an hour later, the two geniuses went back to Great-Grampy Elmer's store to show him their new "shoes." From a distance, they passed for a nice pair of black, wing-tipped shoes.

"Wow, boys, those are nicer than I expected. Good job!" said Great-Grampy Elmer as he walked away satisfied.

The plan was that they'd pick up the girls, Millie and Winnie, at six that evening. They'd walk over the bridge and have some Chinese food at Ming Garden and then walk over to Central Street to The Strand to see the movie. *West of Zanzibar* starring Lon Chaney was playing that night.

The night went off without a hitch. Gramps told me he even got a kiss or two from Millie at the theater.

But things started to go sideways as they walked the girls to their homes. It started to rain. It wasn't a misty, sprinkle rain, but a torrential downpour.

Gramps laughed and told me, "this is the part we didn't plan on."

I asked him what the big deal was, and he laughed again, "well, by the time we got to the other side of the bridge, our paper shoes were nothing more than wet cardboard! The glue seams split. And there we were, Huck and I, walking with black shoe laces and pieces of cardboard hanging on our feet!"

I laughed imagining it. Gramps told me he and Huck had to both work a few more weeks at Great-Grampy Elmer's store as punishment. One week to make up the money for the shoes and the other week for *The Deception* as it was then forever known.

I was never really sure how true Gramps' stories were because they seemed so far-fetched. But every time he told them, the details stayed the same so I'm thinking he wasn't just pulling my leg.

Either way, I didn't mind Sunday mornings at all.

I NAILED IT!

Lately I've realized, reluctantly, that guys can be gross. I'll admit this much. Sometimes though, grossness is necessary—especially, to make a point or settle a bet.

This was the case on the Memorial Day of 1976. It started innocently enough. I was laying on the couch and Mike was sitting on the other end. We were watching *Looney Tunes*. Bugs Bunny in "The Case of the Missing Hare." A classic.

As we watched the cartoon, Mike looked over at my foot and said, "man, your toenails are gross. The big toe looks like you haven't cut it in months!" In retaliation, I took my foot and ran my big toenail down the length of his arm.

"That's friggin' gross. CUT THE CRAP!" he yelled.

Dad walked in the room to tell us off, "shut up, peckerheads. I'm listening to the game out here. Shut up or go outside."

Mike looked at me with a pissed off face.

"My toes aren't gross. I'm seeing how long I can grow them. My goal is to have them curl under," I said.

Never one to walk away from a challenge Mike retorted, "I'll bet I can grow mine longer than you do, but first you have to cut yours now!"

"YOU'RE ON!" I shouted.

Dad came running in the room and yelled, "OUT. NOW!"

I grabbed a plastic bag and the toenail cutters from the bathroom on the way outside. I sat next to him on the porch while I cut my nails and in my best dick voice said, "you are gonna lose, little brutha. My nails grow like weeds!"

"We'll see," he said as he watched me put the clippings into the bag. "Why are you saving them?"

"For motivation, little brutha. Motivation. We will check back with each other three months from today on the last day of summer vacation. That way we'll have plenty of time. The loser has to do the paper route by themselves for a month and give the winner half of the money earned! Deal?"

148

Mike hesitated a moment, making a mental tally of all the cash he could be out if he lost. "Deal," he said. We both spit in our hands and shook on it. Let the Toe Nail Wars begin!

Nothing much was said that first week. We were preoccupied planning our game strategy. I took one of Ma's multivitamins every day. I figured extra vitamins could only help. I noticed Mike was rubbing lotion on his toes before bed and sleeping in socks. Neither of us looked at the other's feet during this time, nor asked how it was coming along. We were saving all conversation for the final reveal.

As the end of the third month came closer, we decided that we'd both meet in the living room with socks on and pull our socks off at the same time to see who won. We'd keep the measuring tape Ma used for sewing on hand in case it was close.

I will admit that my nerves were on edge as I walked into the living room on the fateful day. Dad was in the kitchen again, listening to another game on the radio. We talked in low voices reminding each other that the loser would need to keep their cool or Dad would throw us out on the back porch again.

149

I sat next to Mike and I extended my hand, "may the best man win, brutha." Mike shook my hand and said, "ditto." On the count of three we both pulled off our socks!

Holy shit!

It wasn't even a contest. My nails were long, but Mike's practically curled over! My head was spinning. I didn't understand how they could grow that long in comparison to mine. I sat there with my mouth open and was caught between being pissed off and impressed.

Mike looked at me and smiled. "You should have paid attention to all that Jell-O I ate!" he said.

I realized now, that was my undoing. I had seen him have Jell-O at least twice a day, but I never put two and two together.

He said he went to visit Aunt Agnes, the day after we started our contest, under the guise of a friendly visit, but he really went because she always had really long nails and he wanted to find out her secret.

He told her she had lovely hands. We both knew that was bullshit! She was eighty-eight and her hands were a horrifying mess of veins and wrinkles. Still, she fell for it and told him it was the Jell-O. She said it was like fertilizer for your nails.

I was impressed with his plotting and more than a little pissed off that I hadn't thought of it myself. "Fuck this" I said, "that's kinda cheating. So good luck collecting on this bet!"

Mike stood up and yelled, "DAD, WANNA COME IN HERE FOR A MINUTE?"

I knew then that I was fucked. Dad was, among other things, a man of his word. You made a bet, you lost a bet, you kept your word. *Period.*

Dad came barreling up to me after Mike calmly explained the bet and the outcome and said, "you will do the paper route and you will give your brother half the pay. I'll kick your ass if I find out you give him a penny less! *Understand?*"

I replied that I understood.

Dad turned to leave the room and said over his shoulder, "ya know, you two are a couple of dumbasses! Don't bug me again!"

I scowled at Mike. He smiled and said, "I think I'll keep on growing these out and see how long I can go. Have fun delivering newspapers this month, dinkweed."

I debated whether or not to pop him one, but decided to plot my revenge instead.

I went up to our room and cut off my long nails and added them to the bag of clippings I already had. These would do just fine.

There was an eighth grade dance the following Friday. Being in the seventh grade, Mike needed permission from our parents to go. There was a girl there he liked, so Ma said he could go as long as he walked there with me. When she asked me to bring him, I said sweetly, "not a problem at all, mother."

She looked at me and said, "what are you up to?"

"Me? Why not a thing. Just trying to be a good brother."

Mike was a stickler for laying out his clothes before he put them on. He'd shower then go to the room in his tighty-whities and put on his clothes. He had a tan colored shirt face up, and a pair of jeans already laid out on the bed for the dance. Ironed, with creases down the front of them. While he was in the shower, I ran upstairs to our room with a bottle of glue. I took the bag of nail clippings from my draw and glued five of my toenails on the back of his shirt. Right at the shoulder line. The glue was dry as he finished his usual thirty-minute shower.

"Hey, little brother! I'm glad you are coming tonight. Here let me help you with that shirt so you don't mess up your hair!" I grabbed the shirt and gently helped him get it on over his head.

"Why are you being so nice to me? I thought you'd still be pissed about the bet."

"Bet? What bet? Oh that? Come on. Who cares? I'm over that already," I said.

When we got to the dance, I noticed the toenails blended in nicely with the shirt. It also helped that the lighting was dim.

Mike and I stood on the sidelines with a few of our buddies building up the nerve to ask someone to dance. None of us were into the fast stuff. We were too cool for that.

When "Dream Weaver" played, I knew, being the King of the Dinkweeds, that I'd have to strap on my sack and ask someone to dance or no one else would. I walked up to Jennifer and soon we were snuggling on the dance floor.

Jennifer had a great rack, which was perfect to rest my head upon. At least it was until Mrs. Suketti tapped me on the shoulder with force. She had a red, bouffant hairdo, at least two feet high. As someone who was barely five feet tall, her hair made her look taller.

"Gary, give it some space or they'll be no more slow dancing for you! And Miss Jennifer Glass, what kind of a girl allows a boy to have that kind of access to her bosom? You should be ashamed."

"What kind of a girl? A great one!" I whispered into Jennifer's ear as Ms. Suketti walked away.

She swatted me, pushed me off her chest, and said, "knock it off! Stand up straight—she thinks I'm a whore." I didn't ask her to dance again after this. I figured I knew what the answer would be.

After a few more slow songs, I said to Mike, "get your ass over there and ask Susan to dance. I've seen you looking at her all night! The dance is over in half an hour!"

Mike was shaking as he made his way over to Susan. I stood back watching. She shyly accepted and they walked out to the dance floor. As he and Susan where turning for the third time I noticed them getting a little closer.

Mike leaned in and gave her a little peck on the lips. When he did, Susan did that thing girls do where they ran their hand through the guy's hair. As her hand dropped back down his back, open palmed, it ended up right on the toenails. For a moment she seemed to slow her movements, and then opened her eyes and said loud enough for me to hear, *"What's on the back of your shirt?* IT'S SOMETHING HARD AND SCRATCHY!"

I watched Mike jump back, put his hand over his head, and reach to touch the back of his shirt. He picked at one of the "things" and pulled it forward to look at it! His eyes flew open and he looked over at me then ran out of the dance hall into the bathroom.

While he was in the bathroom, pulling all the nails off, I hightailed it outta there and ran home.

When Mike got home I was already in bed pretending to be asleep. He didn't say a word and

155

went to bed. He was already out with his friends when I woke up the next morning, but he left me a note on my bed that read, "IT IS ON. REVENGE IS SWEET!"

I fear I had woken the sleeping giant!

Over the next few days I decided to lay low and wait for everything to blow over. After a week of nothing happening, I figured he was over it and I forgot about his revenge too.

After dinner, I walked up to my room to get a sweatshirt. I was going over to Ridley Field to get a game of Relievio going. Mike was there when I walked in the room. He quickly and dramatically put his hand behind his back.

"What are you hiding there, little brutha?" I said and pinned him against the wall.

"Nothing," he said.

"Give it over—what is it?" Mike brought his hand forward, and I saw that he held a hand-rolled joint. Mike knew that on occasion, when pressured by peers, I'd occasionally partake in a puff, but I never inhaled. "What are you doing with that?!" I yelled.

Mike said he wasn't going to smoke it, and that he found it outside near Frank's fence. He didn't know what to do with it.

I grabbed it and said, "give it to me, I'll take care of it, and I won't tell Ma you gave it to me." Mike was appreciative and left.

Sometime later, me and two of the guys sat down in Ridley Field and lit up the joint. I'd decided it might upset Ma too much if I gave the pot to her.

I didn't want to upset her since she was such a saint.

I took a long hit, and heard some popping. I kept sucking on it and wasn't getting anything. It smelled like oregano, but something else was giving off a gross burning smell. I stopped smoking, put out the butt, and ripped open the paper. There, mixed in with oregano were toenails. That little prick had made me a toe nail joint!

I enjoyed watching Mike squirm the next few days. I knew he was going crazy wondering how I would retaliate. Three nights later, I passed Mike his bowl of chocolate pudding Ma made for dessert and went to get mine.

We sat down to watch T.V. with Dad, and then Mike took a big bite of pudding and started to cough. He started hacking and drooling, and then stood up and spit out a toenail. I jumped up and ran out the front door while he still was hacking and didn't come back for two hours.

Now it was my turn to squirm.

Over the next two weeks we both walked around like someone was following us. It sucked that I had to keep constantly looking over my shoulder.

Finally, on Sunday morning, I got up early to go deliver the Sunday paper route. It was my last day of having to do it alone. After rolling out of bed, I went downstairs to the bathroom, took a crap, washed my hands, and started to brush my teeth. I felt something scratch against my gums. At first, I thought it was a wayward bristle. It wasn't. I pulled the tooth brush away. Mike had hidden two long toe nails in the bristles.

That was it!

I ran out of the bathroom and bolted up the stairs. I grabbed Mike, still sleeping, out of his bed. "You son-of-a-bitch! That's it, that's the last time! It ends now! *Okay*?"

"Okay," he said.

"Give me your bag and I'll give you mine and we swear on great Grandpa Elmer's grave—NO MORE!"

I pulled him up and we both grabbed our bags of nails, and I said, "let's go flush them."

We went downstairs and flushed them down the toilet. This summer would go down in history as The Summer of the Toe Nails.

We both had a new-found respect for each other. Even though I was still the King of the Dinkweeds, Mike had become my second in command. Not just a brother but a friend, and a cool one at that! That was a good thing, and this was a good summer.

THE CARSON SISTERS

Walking home late one summer night, I saw Mary and Angie sitting on their front steps. This wasn't unusual to see in the summer. Their folks, like mine, would let us stay out on the front steps as long as they were awake. Our parents felt the same —it was better to let us outside than to put up with us bitching about how hot it was.

I stopped by my house and yelled through the screen door to let Ma know I was going to sit with Angie and Mary.

I asked them what they were up to and sat down on their front steps. I could tell they had walked to the corner store earlier because they were reading "rag mags" and snacking on pumpkin seeds and cold Cokes.

Angie filled me in on the latest Hollywood gossip, but then Mary interrupted and said, "it gives me the shivers whenever I look across the street at the Carson house. I heard that Ethel was convicted of murder."

The Carson sisters had lived on our street longer than anyone else in the neighborhood. They were two old ladies alone. Ethel was deaf and crabby, and Anna didn't say much. Whenever we set a foot on their sidewalk or lawn, Ethel would come out, with a sickle in her hand and stare at you till you got off her property.

They never had any lights on in the house, and once in a while we heard Anna playing the piano. It was creepy as hell.

Angie was the only one in the neighborhood allowed on their property. She was never allowed in the house—no one was—but she was allowed to walk their sidewalk or sometimes sit on their steps.

"Ang, why do they like you? Why do you like them? Don't they give you the creeps?"

"No, they're just old, but they're nice," she said. "Once Ethel saw me picking blackberries in Mrs. Moran's yard. I offered her my cup and she went inside her house. When she came back out, the cup was full of fresh cherries. Ever since then she liked me and I've liked her."

"Well she gives me the creeps," I said. "I mean, why does she have to come out with a sickle like she's gonna chop our heads off. It's weird. Especially with everyone saying she was a murderer."

"Those are just rumors, Gary," Angie said.

We sat and talked a little while longer until Mr. Martin came to the door. "Okay, gang. Time to wrap it up. Me and Mrs. Martin are ready for bed." We all said our good nights and I went back home.

Dad was in bed, but Ma was up sitting in her rocker and knitting. *The Great Entertainment* was on, and Frank Avruch introduced the movie *Daddy Long Legs* starring Fred Astaire.

I grabbed some lemonade and sat next to Ma in Dad's chair. "Ma, what do you know about the Carson sisters?" I started right away.

She stopped knitting and said, "you leave those old ladies alone. God knows, they've had their hardships."

It took some pressing, but eventually she caved and explained what "hardships" the Carson sisters had been through. "Years ago, long before we moved in, Anna used to live there with her husband and her

162

sister, Ethel. One day, she came home from the market and the police were at her door waiting for her. They told her that while she was out, Ethel had gone downstairs to put more coal in the stove. Instead she found Anna's husband. He was dead. It seemed like he shot himself. Since Ethel was deaf, she didn't hear anything.

Shortly after, Anna had a nervous breakdown and spent some time in a hospital. Ethel was never the same after that. She became nervous and reclusive. People started talking and spreading rumors that Ethel killed him because she was jealous of Anna's relationship. I don't believe that though. As I said, they've been through enough. Don't bother them. I mean it."

Of course, when I got up to bed I told Mike first thing. Aaron was sound asleep, and Mike and I sat on the floor talking about how much we wanted to have a peek inside that house. Just a quick look around. I seemed to want it a little more than Mike, but I knew he'd go along with whatever plan I came up with.

About a week after I talked with Angie and Mary on their front steps, Anna was standing at our fence calling out to my mother. Ma came out and Anna told her that Ethel had passed away sometime in the night before last and she needed us to call someone.

Ethel had been dead an entire day at this point, and when the medical examiner and the undertaker stopped by they kept coming outside gagging. Mr. Kennedy, the undertaker, told Ma he'd never seen anyone living in such horrible conditions. He said they had no running water and would empty their crap outside into their backyard. It was a sad situation, and I felt bad for them.

Some of the neighbors came outside to see what was going on. I saw Angie crying when they took Ethel out. Shortly after, they mentioned that they were relocating Anna to a nursing home and condemning the house. Angie cried then too.

A few neighbors complained that they wanted the house ripped down right away. I overheard Dad talking to Ma that night, "you *know* how long those city bastards will take. They don't give a shit if that house is an eyesore as long as they aren't looking at it." He was right. The Carson's house sat there for almost a year before the "city bastards" were forced to demolish it.

I say "forced" because a week before it was taken down, Mike and I decided it was a good time to take a peek inside. We waited until our folks went food shopping one Saturday morning. I'm not ashamed to admit that we were both too chicken to go in the house at night.

As soon as Ma and Dad turned the corner of the street and were out of sight, Mike and I snuck around the back of the house.

By now, the smell of crap and piss had faded. When we got to the door, we saw that someone had already moved the board covering the door. Mike smiled nervously at me.

It was easy to slip inside the house.

We came in through the kitchen. It was old and dusty, and I felt like we were in a time warp. They had one of those old washing machines and a well pump at the sink.

We made our way to the next room. It was the living room. There was an old, dusty couch and the piano we'd sometimes hear Anna playing. Everything was covered in dust and cobwebs.

I was ahead of Mike as we made our way around the corner to the stairs that would bring us up to the second floor. I stopped dead in my tracks. It took my brain a second to process what I was looking at. And then I realized.

I immediately spun around, grabbed Mike, and put my hands over his eyes. He yelled and scrambled to get away from me, "what are you doing? LET GO!"

I pulled him back and told him he didn't want to see or know and we needed to get the hell out of the house. I knew he thought I was being a dick and trying to scare him, but I didn't care. We had to get out. We ran outside and back home as fast as we could.

Ma had just come home with Dad as I rushed over and told her. She quickly called the cops.

A few months earlier, Walter Ennis, this troubled kid from a few streets over, went missing. He was bad news, and he always seemed to be in trouble with the law. Not that he deserved what happened to him… One day, he never came home. His parents put signs all over the neighborhood, but no one ever found him.

The police confirmed later on that day that I had seen Walter Ennis hanging from the banister over the staircase. The medical examiner determined that he had been there *at least* a month.

It didn't take long for the city to come in and tear down the house after that.

Ma and Dad talked to me and asked if I wanted "see someone" to talk about what I saw that day. I didn't want to. To be honest, I was grateful Mike hadn't seen Walter hanging there. He flipped once after catching a glimpse of the poster for *The Exorcist*. I think this would have wrecked him.

Dad had the same idea.

A few weeks later, on my way to bed, he called me outside as I walked by the front screen door. He was sitting on our front steps and drinking a beer. He motioned for me to sit down with him.

We sat there in silence for a few minutes, and then he took a big gulp of beer. He looked over at me, jerked his head towards the empty lot across the street, and said, "buddy, I'm proud of you covering your little brother's eyes. That's not something he needs to see…You didn't need to see it either, Gary, but you're like me, kid. Tough. You'll be alright."

He handed me his beer and made a "go ahead" gesture. I took a big swig, and Dad put his arm around my shoulders, "this is just between us men. Don't tell your mother!"

I never did.

SNOW DAYS

Aaron loved snow days. He loved the surprise of them, and he'd tell Ma to trick us whenever we had one. So, when she heard that our school was closed, she would still wake us up, make us get dressed, and wouldn't tell us school was closed until we walked out the door.

This would piss Mike off, "*cripes*, Ma, you could have let us sleep in!"

But not Aaron. He'd be so giddy he'd literally dance a jig around the house.

I acted like I didn't give a shit either way. But what kid doesn't like it when school is cancelled? Any excuse to stay home was fine with me.

I was always amazed by the amount of energy Aaron would have as soon as Ma told us we didn't have to go to school. It was like a switch flipped in his brain and he'd transform from a cranky, tired, little shit to a happy, energetic elf in a second.

He'd start making Snow Day Plans. The three of us would get all bundled up, go outside to the backyard, and start making an igloo. The igloo was always first on the list.

Each of us had a side to complete. We'd pack the snow down hard and high. In the end, each side was about four feet tall (The Blizzard of '78 produced our biggest igloo). Each wall had to have a small window in the center so that we could see out once the snowball fights started.

After the three walls were done we'd all work together building a "snowball wall." We'd crank out snow balls for ammo and pile them up into high mounds.

When that was finished, we'd walk up to the corner store together and get some peanut butter cups and tonics. We bury them in the walls of the igloo because nothing is better than a freezing bottle of Coca-Cola and frozen peanut butter cups.

Then the fight would begin. We'd spend the rest of the day with our buddies fighting a neighborhood-wide snowball fight.

Living in New England, we had a ton of snow days and snowball fights, but one snowball fight stands out in my mind. It was different because it involved Angie and the Rooney's.

That day, all twelve of us met in my yard to split up into teams. We were going to play Relievio-Snowball. It was the same idea as a usual game of Relievio, but this time, instead of tagging people, we'd hit them with a snowball. If it landed, they were caught until someone from their team relieved them.

Angie showed up with her friend from the end of the street, Donna Rooney. Donna and Angie hung out quite a bit. I didn't know Donna that well, but she seemed okay.

When we were gearing up to get started, Mrs. Rooney came out on her front steps, put her two fingers to her mouth, and gave a loud whistle. Angie and Donna froze and then Angie said, "we have to go in for a second. Real quick. We'll be right back. Don't start without us!"

They came back out ten minutes later and we were sure to let them know how pissed we were to have to wait for them. The game was on!

I was captain of one team and Kyle led the other one. Even though I got stuck with Angie and Donna on my team, I had Mitch and both of my brothers. Mike and Aaron were aces when it came to Relievio, and they were great at chucking snowballs. Because they learned from the master, obviously.

As usual, we kicked ass.

After spending sometime gloating about our win, the group split up and everyone made their way home. Donna said good night and I was left walking with Angie.

"Hey, not for nothing, but it was kinda weird how Mrs. Rooney whistled and you two took off running. What's up with that?" I asked.

"Oh yeah, sorry about that. We had to sit on Mr. Rooney," she answered.

"What? You had to *sit* on Mr. Rooney? What the hell are you talking about?" My mind raced—I'd kill that son-of-a-bitch if this ended up being something pervy.

But before I could say anything else, Angie cut in, "well, it's Friday, so we had to sit on him." She said this like it explained everything.

I stopped her at this point, and I motioned for her to come sit down next to me on the curb in front of our houses. "Ang, tell me what you mean by 'it's Friday and we had to sit on Mr. Rooney.' I mean, *what the hell* does that even mean?"

"Oh okay. Well, Mr. Rooney has a drinking problem. He drinks all night and every night when he comes home from work. He gets paid on Fridays. Mrs. Rooney needs his paycheck and sometimes, 'cause he's drunk, he gives her a hard time about handing it over. So, she wrestles him to the ground, and me and Donna have to sit on him while she goes through his pockets to get the check."

I sat there a few minutes looking at her and picturing this visual in my head. "How long has this been going on?"

"I don't know, since last winter, I think. We weren't heavy enough before then," she said matter-of-factly.

"Hey Ang, you know that's totally fucked up, right?"

"I never really thought about it before," she said as she got up from the curb, "I wanna go in now, Gary, my bum is cold. Good snowball fight today."

I sat there a few more minutes and watched her go inside. Her dad would shit if he knew Mrs. Rooney was having her do that.

Mr. Rooney lived another ten years after that night Angie and I talked on the curb. Years later, I asked Angie how long the Rooney's "wrestling match" had gone on. She told me it lasted until their sophomore year of high school, and only ended because Donna crushed on this boy who liked Angie instead.

It led to a fight, and Angie told me she told Donna, "I don't even like him back so I don't know what your problem is."

Then, Donna told her they were done being friends and not to bother sitting on Mr. Rooney with her anymore because she'd "find someone else."

Angie said that it really hurt her feelings.

I laughed and told her, "I stand by what I said to you the night you first told me, Ang. That's all kinds of fucked up!"

She just smiled and said, "you think so?"

174

PASTOR JAMES

Russell's father was the Pastor of the Baptist church in our neighborhood. He was also blind. Ma called him a "saintly man." I never really talked to him much because he was never home when Russ and I hung out after school. Every night though, after dinner, I'd see him walking down the street with his cane on his way home.

One summer day, when we were bored and looking for things to do, Mark came up with an idea. He had older brothers who bought dirty girlie books from Victor's Variety on Main Street. Seeing where he was headed, I told Mark that we weren't stealing books from his brothers—they would kick our asses.

Everyone agreed, and Mark came up with another idea. "Gary, the lady who works the counter, Blanche, has a crush on your dad. We can use that to our advantage."

It was common knowledge in the neighborhood. I'd seen it myself. Blanche lit up every Sunday after mass when we'd go into the store with Dad. She acted flirty and sweet.

I told him once when we left the store, "Dad, it's kinda gross, but I think Blanche likes you or something."

He smiled and said, "well, your Ma has nothing to worry about."

Mark said we should go into Victor's and have me distract Blanche with a story about my Dad while the others snagged a few books.

This sounded great, but I told the guys there was one problem. "Where are we supposed to read these books?" Everyone knew this was an issue. My brothers were pains-in-the-ass and would never leave us alone in the cellar. The other guys had similar situations as well. Ridley Field was out because if any of the other guys that hung there saw us, they'd want in on it too and that'd be a pain.

Then Russell told us he had another idea. An *awesome* idea. He mentioned that there was a lot of leftover siding and wood in his yard from work his parents had done on the house. He explained that his Ma was complaining about the mess.

That night, he went home to his parents and asked if he could make a fort in the backyard with the leftover wood. He made a great case to his folks, "I feel like this is something I need to do myself to prove that I can do it all alone. It'll be great for my self-esteem." He told us later that he had them eating out of his hands when he added, "my self-esteem has taken a hit lately. I feel depressed."

That's all his mother needed to hear, "God, help him, Pastor. We can't let that be the case."

The Pastor thought this would be a great idea on Russ' path to becoming a man and said he could as long as he let his brother go into the fort once in a while.

Russ promised, but crossed his fingers behind his back. He had no intention of letting Rick come into the fort, especially when us guys were hanging in there.

Russell got started the next morning. We were all anxious and wanted to help but he said he had to do it alone or his folks would know he was up to something.

It took him a week to build the fort. It came out pretty nice. He lined the floor with leftover carpet pieces, and he ran an extension cord and hung up a

177

strand of Christmas lights. It was our own fortress of solitude.

That night, we all met in the fort to go over the plan. His mom agreed to let us have a camp out. It was a nice summer night. Rick was staying at his grandparents' house for the week so it worked out great.

I came prepared for this camp out. Earlier, I took an empty bottle of olive oil and cleaned it out. I filled it with the whiskey I had nicked from Dad's black box of confiscated goods. I replaced his whiskey with water so I wouldn't upset him.

All of us hunkered down in our sleeping bags, passing around the whiskey and outlining our plan for the following morning. We figured we would do it on an early weekday morning for a few reasons. First, most people were at work so there would be less grownups around. And second, who reads porn that early? No one would pay attention to that section of the store.

We all fell asleep satisfied with the plan and slightly buzzed.

We woke up to the smell of bacon and to the sound of Mrs. James yelling out the back door, "boys, there are eggs and bakey, wakey wakey."

We all let her idiot remark slide because we were hungry. As we ate she asked what was on our agenda for today. Russell told her we were going to have a baseball tournament at the park all morning and wouldn't be back until later.

She said she'd be off running errands and visiting her sister, and she reminded Russ of the number to call if he needed her for anything.

After breakfast, he grabbed his baseball hat and we took off.

The four of us walked into the store ten minutes after it opened. You could smell the fresh coffee that Blanche had made and the donuts. It was time to go.

I walked up to the counter and watched Blanche arrange the donuts. The other guys were already walking around trying to act like they were looking at other things. The dirty books were down the end in their own little section labeled "Must be 18 years or older." I saw Russ slowly make his way over to the magazine section out of the corner of my eye.

179

I started talking to Blanche, "boy, those donuts sure do smell good!"

"Only ten cents each, Gary. Want one?"

"Sure, give me a glazed."

As she picked up the wax paper and started to grab the donut I said, "you know Blanche, my dad mentioned you the other night."

She almost dropped the donut. "He did? Me? Well, why, what did he say?" Her face was bright red and I had her full attention.

"Well, we were just talking about what a nice lady you were, ya know, 'cause we see you every week after church and everything, and he said, 'yeah, she is,' then he said, 'if I wasn't married...'"

"What? *Really*? Wow, that's funny."

I told her I guess he thought she was pretty or something. She was all flustered and I saw Russ walk out of the store. It was good timing because I was running out of bullshit to sling.

Mark and Tommy came up to the counter and they both bought a donut. After they paid I told Blanche to have a nice day.

"You too, Gary, and please tell your dad I said 'hello!'" she said with a big smile. I told her I would and we left.

When we got outside Russ put his finger to his lips and held up three fingers. We all saw the bulge under his windbreaker. None of us said a word as we walked back to the fort.

The next few days, every free second we got we spent in the fort. The four of us huddled around the books. We thought we were brilliant, evil geniuses. We took the books, got away with it, and enjoyed the fruits of our thievery.

Looking at the books was great, but our hard-ons were being wasted. We decided that we could each take one picture out of the books to bring home. None of us needed to say why, but we all knew.

The next week, Rick came home from his grandparents. He kept hounding us to come into the fort but Russ kept telling him no. After four days of this, as we were eyeballing Miss July, Pastor James barged into the fort. We all froze. I saw the panic in Russ' eyes. We didn't even have time to hide the books.

181

Everyone was panicking, but I made a shushing motion and pointed to my eyes. We all sat there in silence until Russ said, "hey, Dad. What's up?"

Pastor James stood there and said, "hello, boys. Are all four of you in here?"

I piped up, "yes, sir, it's nice to see you today."

Pastor James smiled and joked, "well I can't say the same, but nice to hear from you, Gary. So, what are you boys doing out here?"

"Just hanging around, Dad," Russ said.

"Fine boys, that's just fine," the Pastor answered.

He made a move like he was going to leave but then turned back and said, "oh boys, by the way, why don't you hand me those pornographic magazines you have there? I need to find out where you got them." We all froze again.

Tommy immediately caved. He stood up and shouted, "WE STOLE THEM FROM VICTOR'S."

What a moron.

I wanted to punch him in the head, but to tell the truth, the Pastor was very intimidating. I might have cracked too. He told us to follow him out onto the lawn. It seems Rick did some snooping and ratted us out for not letting him come into the fort.

My Ma likes to tell this part of the story whenever it comes up. She always starts with how she was talking to Mrs. Martin at the corner store. Then, she goes on about how she got the biggest kick out of seeing Pastor James and the four of us marching down Main Street in single file. We were on our way to return the stolen goods and confess our sins to Blanche.

Blanche was very understanding. "Well, boys will be boys, I guess." She also barred us from the store for a month unless we were accompanied by one of our parents. We got off pretty easy.

As for the Pastor, he put us to work cleaning the church for four Saturdays in a row. We washed windows, dusted, and did all the cleaning tasks he could think of to repent for our sins.

We never knew what happened to the books we turned in, and no one ever came after us about missing pages we each tore out. That'll be three "Our Father's" and three "Hail Mary's."

HOPELESSLY DEVOTED

It was a Saturday like any other. I woke up at about ten o'clock, threw on a pair of Levi's that had been in a ball at the foot of my bed, and grabbed a cup of coffee to sit on the back porch.

While I sat mulling over how I wanted to spend the day, I noticed Aaron in the side yard with a big piece of poster board, a long stick, and markers.

"What are you up to, dinkweed?"

Without looking up at me he said, "Angie and her friends are bugging me. Last week, they started a Women's Lib Club. They made buttons, listened to that 'I am Woman' song, and spent the day talking about how much they hate guys. Me and my buddies are making our own signs to see how they like it."

I chuckled. I gotta hand it to Aaron, he's was always a little shit, but he's never been afraid to speak up. The kid has a set of balls on him.

After a few minutes, I got up to refill my cup, I decided to sit on the front steps to see what was going on in the neighborhood. I found Dad out front watering our little patch of grass and the roses he had planted. My Old Man had a green thumb. Ma said he liked to plant things because it reminded him of growing up in the country.

As he watered the grass, he said without looking at me, "make sure you eat something. I don't need you all hopped up on only caffeine and bugging me on my day off!"

"No problem, Pop. I'll eat in a few." Then, I asked, "hey, why aren't you working at all today? Don't you have to go to the nursing home later or something?"

"No, I took the whole day off because I'm burnt out. Tonight, we're all going to the drive-in with the Martins. So, don't make any plans. We're gonna see that *Grease* picture Ma has been talking about."

"Sure thing, Dad."

Dad hung around for a bit, but then he went back inside. I was still outside when I saw three of Aaron's friends walk down the street with signs. They asked if Aaron was awake and I pointed them to the side yard.

"Hey, Aaron, ya ready?" they asked from the street. Aaron walked through the gate and handed his sign to a friend.

185

Then, he went to the Martin's house next door and asked for Angie. Angie came to the door with her friend, Donna. They were both in their pajamas.

"What do you want, Aaron?" she asked. Aaron ran back out of their yard, grabbed his sign, and all the guys proceeded to walk in a circle in front of her house. They had posters that had pictures of witches they had drawn with arrows pointing to the word "GIRLS." It was all written in big, red letters.

They chanted while they marched. "THIS IS TRUE! THIS IS TRUE!"

Angie got red in the face and said, "you guys are a bunch of jerks!" She slammed her front door shut.

"Good one, numbnuts!" I called to Aaron. "We have to go to the drive-in with her and her family tonight. She's gonna be pissed at you all night now!"

"*CRAP*," he said. "Okay, boys. I think we made our point. Let's go hang out at Ridley Field."

With that, they threw their signs over the fence and all ran up the street. I just shook my head and went in for some breakfast. I felt like today would make a good lazy day.

After dinner, Ma loaded up the red and white Coleman cooler with cherry Kool-Aid and a big, paper bag full of popcorn. I could see the grease stains from the butter bleeding through the bag. She told us to grab our sleeping bags and get into the station wagon.

Michael and Aaron yelled out, "we call the way back," and they jumped into the seat that faced the opposite direction from everyone else.

"Hey, numbnuts, you don't need to call it out! I don't want it. You look like morons anyway. I mean, you're staring at the people in the cars behind us! Don't you feel stupid just sitting there looking at them?" I said.

"Way to make us feel self-conscious, Gary. Thanks a lot!" said Mike.

"Yeah, mind your own business and *stop aggravating with us!*" yelled Aaron.

"SHUT UP, PECKERHEADS. STOP TALKING!" Dad yelled back. The car went quiet and we were on our way.

It cost five bucks to get a car in the Rt. 22 drive-in. We parked next to the Martins.

187

After we parked, everyone scrambled to set up and get a good spot to watch the movie. Mike and Aaron grabbed their sleeping bags and got up on the roof of the car. Angie and Donna did the same on the Martin's station wagon. Ma, Dad, and Mr. and Mrs. Martin all grabbed lawn chairs and put them between the two cars. Dad set up the silver speakers attached to the poles so we could hear the movie.

That just left me and Mary in our own cars. About fifteen minutes into the movie, there was a knock on my window. I rolled it all the way down and Mary asked if I wanted to take a walk with her to get some fries at the snack bar.

After sharing some fries and a Coke, we walked over to the outdoor park attached to the drive-in. We each hopped on a swing.

"Is Angie still pissed at Aaron?" I asked Mary.

"No, she forgot about it as soon as Dad said she could bring Donna tonight. That whole fight they were having is stupid. I told her so."

We rocked back and forth on our swings talking and only half paying attention to the movie. That changed when Olivia Newton John came on screen in her white nightgown. She started to sing "Hopelessly Devoted to You." They've been playing it on the radio a lot since the movie came out.

"Oh man, I love this song!" Mary said.

"I don't know," I countered.

"Cut it out. You like it too!" she teased.

"I don't know, Mar. I mean, it's okay, I guess."

"Come on, Gary, you like it, I mean you have to! You are so hopelessly devoted to me!" she said as she laughed.

She reached over to swat me. I grabbed her hand and looked at her and said, "maybe I am."

"Very funny, Gary," she said as she started to pull her hand away.

I pulled her hand closer to me, pulling her swing up against mine and I said, "no, really, maybe I am Mar. I mean, maybe I've always been."

Mary just looked at me, her blue eyes sparkling in the moonlight, "really?" she whispered.

"Really," I answered.

As we sat on the swings kissing under the blanket of stars while Olivia Newton John belted out

"Hopelessly Devoted to You," I thought, I'm getting the best girl in the neighborhood.

Maybe I'm not such a dick after all.

EPILOGUE

Years have passed since I've lived in that old neighborhood. I still keep in touch with some of my friends from those days but not all of them. Some moved on, some died. My brothers and Angie moved away and are all happily married to great people.

I have a home in the suburbs now, and I make a good living. We have two boys, Danny and Raymond. Mary is a great wife and we have built a nice life for ourselves.

The funny part is that I work fifteen minutes from our old neighborhood and have to drive by the street every day.

I rarely take that ride down though.

After Dad passed away, we knew it was time for Ma to move out. The neighborhood had gone downhill. City life and drug deals had finally caught up to it.

Ma reluctantly agreed to move and we all came home one last time to remember the house that built us. Those walls will forever hold our memories and our hearts.

Sometimes, in the summer, in my quiet house, with my quiet life, if the breeze is right I can still smell the stinkweed that used to grow in the back of the Carson sisters' house. I miss the hot summer nights I spent listening to the traffic on Bridge Street with the windows thrown open as the curtains blew in from the summer breeze.

I remember staying up and waiting for *Saturday Night Live* to end so that we could watch the *Midnight Special* with Wolfman Jack and see if any of our favorite singers would be on that week. I long for the city noise at night and wish we didn't have central air. Mary feels the same. We will never have times like that again. Now, we can only hope that we can pass some of the good, old time childhood memories onto our privileged kids.

This morning after the 8:30 mass, Mary and I decided to take the boys on a trip down memory lane. I told them about Ridley Field as we drove slowly down our old street. I told them how we went sledding in the winter and played Relievio in the summer. Now, Ridley Field is a pizza parlor.

Next, I pointed out the pear tree that was still behind the house across the street from my old home. I told them how we used to pick blackberries and rhubarb there, sitting in the un-mowed grass with cups of sugar to dip the fruit in. I pointed to the lot that used to be the Carson sister's house. It's now mostly a pile of rubble.

Then I showed them our house. I told them about the porch my brothers and I would sit out on. I pointed out the bedroom window that used to be my parents' room and reminded them how we'd all camp out on the floor in the summer with the one air conditioner.

Mary pointed out her house next door. I mentioned how I used to watch her in her bikini on her roof when she sunbathed. I left out a few details.

Mary and I sat there for a while stuck in our memories, remembering the feelings and smells so thick you could cut them with a knife. Then our youngest, Raymond, pulled us back to reality.

"Geez, you guys lived in a crappy, poor neighborhood!"

Before I had a chance to say something, to let him know how pissed I was that he wasn't *getting it,* Danny piped up and said to Raymond, "shut up, ya little dinkweed, or I belt ya one!"

Mary nudged me and I smiled. Everything had come full circle, and all was right with the world.

ACKNOWLEDGEMENTS

I'd like to send a quick shout out to my besties, Tam and Keith, who read each chapter first. Thank you for your patience and encouragement!

Thank you to my husband who listened to these stories on our car rides. His laughter and nostalgic responses kept me moving forward.

Again, I'd like to thank my siblings for giving me these memories and something to do to occupy this menopausal woman's time.

Also, a big thank you to Liz Rufiange for editing this book. I hope my reminders that it was a young guy talking were helpful!

ABOUT THE AUTHOR

Amy Reidy was born in Lowell, Massachusetts. Even though she currently lives in New Hampshire, she will always be a Lowell girl at heart.

She feels that she has been blessed with the world's greatest family and is grateful for her siblings, in-laws, friends, and dogs (R.I.P. Josie). She considers the health, happiness, and success of her children, their partners, her husband, and grandchildren among her greatest accomplishments in life.

In her spare time, she enjoys playing the piano. She also can play a song on the tin whistle and harmonica. She loves photography and took a photo that won the "Editor's Pick" in *National Geographic*. Amy also spends her time painting, cooking, and counting down the days until Halloween. She has also published two words in Urban Dictionary ("dickscapade" and "squeenge beef").

Her best piece of advice is this: "it's easy to forget what's important in life...so don't!"

Never give up and remember, it's never too late!

Made in the USA
Lexington, KY
07 December 2019